Lies of the Land

the truth of the matter

By Dick Hoskins

Polecat Press
Coeur d' Alene, Idaho

Cover by Jackie Oldfield, Keokee Co. Publishing

Drawings by Steve Parker

Copyright © 1998 by William R. Hoskins

Library of Congress Catalog Card number 98-92070

ISBN 0-9639816-3-3

Table of Contents

Introduction

Alas, there are *so* many liars in this world, and *so* many lies being passed around. If you find yourself thinking, as you read this book, "I've heard that one before," please look back at my sub-title. I've attempted to right a serious wrong by telling the *true* story behind some of these lies. Pat McManus says the truth slips in, no matter how one tries to keep it out, but I've done my best to round it up and corral it in totally truthful stories. Some of these lies are true, some aren't. You decide which are which.

If you have read my previous books, you will find some old friends in this one: my long-suffering wife, The O'Reilly; my little bulldog, Snooks; H. B. Miller, a hero to me in my youth; and Old Bill Kittmeister, an anti-hero of sorts. Of course, Dowd and Murdie appear as my cohorts in crime. And don't forget that walking catastrophe-waiting-to-happen, Elroy Blurch.

Another thing you will find, every now and again, is someone quoted as saying, "For pity's sake." You may substitute your own words. The source of this "swear" word is this family joke:

Two telephone linemen were working on a pole when their supervisor drove up.

"Say," he said. "A lady who lives right near here complained about the language you guys are using."

"Us? We haven't said anything out of line."

"You haven't said anything at all?"

"Well, I guess I did say something when Pete dropped hot solder off the pole down my neck."

"Well, what did you say?"

"Oh, I said, 'For pity's sake, Pete, please be more careful.'"

Well, *I* thought it was funny.

A True Story

Things are not always what they seem.

The loss of his only son to diphtheria in 1930 devastated Ernie. His wife could never have another child, and every man wants a son to "carry on the name." Depressed and angry at God, Ernie sought solitude in the Mission Mountains. His wife, equally bereaved, begged him not to go. They had just buried the boy in the orchard near the house, and the neighbors had not heard of the tragedy, else they would have come to comfort her. In his anger, Ernie ignored her and left for the mountains.

In the fine summer weather, Ernie explored the higher parts of the mountains, along the bases of the glaciers which then filled many of the upper valleys. Following the base of the Mt. MacDonald glacier, he came upon some ravens feasting. As he approached, the scavengers flew away, leaving bones Ernie recognized as human. When he examined the bones, he found part of the corpse still under the ice, and he realized that this was a human who had frozen in the glacier many years before, and his body was only then being released by the retreating ice. Looking up at the ice front he saw, covered by only a few inches of ice, a small body he recognized as that of a young boy. His recent loss in mind, he vowed, as he stood there, to keep this boy before him from the repulsive scavengers and to give him a decent (his bitterness and anger kept him from even *thinking* "Christian") burial. He took up the miner's pick he always carried and chipped away at the ice. Near dark, he finally freed the small body. He decided to wait until morning light to choose a grave site, so he built a good fire to warm himself from the glacier's cold and settled down for the night. Some time later, he thought he heard a whimper. He looked beyond the

1

firelight but could see no varmint there, so he built up the fire and settled down again. Before long he dreamed he heard his dead son crying. He shook himself loose from the dream and realized the crying was real. The small boy whimpered and shivered near the fire. Ernie was, of course, thunderstruck. Had he been Catholic, he would, no doubt, have crossed himself and recited a prayer. As it was, he hesitated, then approached the child fearfully. The boy reached out for him, and immediately they were crying in each other's arms. Evidently the warm fire had melted his frozen charge, and the boy was crying from the cold he could now feel. The boy spoke words Ernie could not understand, although they seemed to him to resemble Norse words. He moved the small body closer to the fire, and massaged the tiny arms and legs until warmth flooded them.

In the light of day, Ernie examined his charge. The boy was fair and blue-eyed with brown hair. Just like his lost son. The boy's build was slight. Just like his lost son. He had found a new purpose. This child would live, and replace the child Ernie had lost.

Ernie hurried down the mountain and took the child home. No one must know. The child took the place of his dead son, and replaced him in every way. He learned to speak as his father spoke, and his early accent was easily explained away as an effect of the diphtheria.

The strange clothing the boy wore when he was found intrigued Ernie. Although roughly made, it bore little resemblance to that of any Indian tribe in the vicinity. Besides, the blue-eyed boy was obviously not one of the First People. Ernie finally assembled enough nerve to ask for help from his sister who taught school in Iowa. He sent the clothing to her, only telling her that he had found it in the mountains. She took it to experts at museums in Des

Moines, who also were puzzled. She even made a special trip to Chicago, and asked the curators there. They assured her the clothing could not have come from the Montana mountains—it appeared to be Viking in origin, and well over a thousand years old, although they marveled at how well it had been preserved. Perhaps, they said, it was a very good and carefully made forgery. Ernie knew it was no fake. The boy was a Viking survivor who had somehow come all the way across the continent.

I know this story is true—Ernie told it all to me shortly before he died.

Now I understand something that bothered me for years. In the Navy, my best buddy was a Norwegian from North Dakota. When he grew depressed—"rock happy," we called it—he got mad easily, particularly at me. He'd cuss me in English until he ran out of words, then switch to Norwegian. I always wondered why I understood every cuss-word he said. Now I know.

Thanks, Ernie, for being a great Dad to a Viking waif.

So you see, things are not always what they seem. I appear to you as a young man of seventy years or so. In truth, I must be nearly twelve hundred years old.

Gophers

In several places in this book you will read about my experiences with "gophers," so I'll tell you more about them than you want to know. The ubiquitous critters we called gophers when I was a tad are really, I found out long after I left home, Columbian ground squirrels, and are found throughout the dry areas of the Pacific Northwest. They are a subspecies of the common ground squirrel, and get their name from their range; the Columbia Plateau, or the drainage of the Columbia River.

City-dwelling animal lovers think the little animals are "cute" and that the methods we used to control them were cruel and inhumane. Perhaps they were, but when we were scrabbling to make a living in the 1930s and 40s we saw the situation as "us or them." I guess we won. When I go back to the Flathead now, I seldom see a gopher.

Sixty years ago, colonies of gophers were everywhere. To satisfy their voracious appetites, they stripped the vegetation for a goodly distance around each colony, and their holes were a menace to farm animal legs—hence our constant war on them. The coming of irrigation drowned the gophers out of the level ground and forced them to the slightly higher ground of dry knolls and ditch banks. We did our best to keep them confined there.

Once in a while we found a gopher hole in a field where we could divert irrigation water into it, and my dog Snooks had great sport catching the half-drowned varmints as they came out. Once I flooded a hole that housed a family of half a dozen young gophers, and she had her hands more than full. She stopped her sport long enough to look accusingly at me as if to say, "Enough,

4

already. Stop sending them." Then she was off after a gopher that almost got away.

Snooks also liked to go hunting with me. When I got out the .22 she danced around as if on springs, because she knew there was sport involved. I was a fair shot and when I knocked a gopher down, Snooks was right on it to finish off the kill, whether or not her ministrations were needed. Her eagerness sometimes precluded getting a shot at another gopher before they all went to ground. Sometimes we went on to another colony; sometimes we waited until those in this colony popped up again. Often even Snooks and I could out-wait the gophers, and I could get three or four shots from a stand in the course of a half hour.

Gopher hunting also gave us boys an excuse to take our Sunday afternoon dates to a secluded area. There were numerous knolls in less densely populated areas where a boy and a girl could sit together behind the rocks pretending they were waiting for a gopher to show his head. The girl usually was willing to wait, even though there was no gopher colony in sight.

Farmers took drastic measures with the gophers when they became too numerous. For a time we tried poisoning the little varmints—using barley provided, I believe, by the County Extension Agent. We placed the poisoned grain carefully down in the hole so the pheasants and other animals couldn't get to it. What no one understood, at first, was that poisoned gophers were a danger to the farm dogs and cats.

We abandoned poisoned grain for poison gas. I'm not sure where we got it, but we used a powder which, when combined with water, generated cyanide gas. One carried the powder and a bucket of water, dumped a little powder below the entrance of a gopher hole, poured a little water

5

on the powder, then sealed the hole quickly. I seldom was able to seal the hole without getting a whiff of cyanide. Olfactory memories, they say, are the best retained. I can dredge up the odor of cyanide more than sixty years later.

Something is gone from the valley now. I miss the whistle of the ground squirrel, and miss seeing him sitting ramrod straight on watch by his hole. Good grief! Am I becoming an environmentalist?

Dirty Trick

Fishing was poor, so we all returned to camp early, had some stew, then started a poker game in one of the larger tents. After a few hours of poker and a few beers, I needed to find the "facilities" and then a bunk. In the high mountains, the facilities include almost anywhere, so after I found a spot off the main path, I sought my tent. I needed a snack before going to bed and a peanut butter sandwich sounded just right. I crawled into the truck, got out the peanut butter and some bread and began to dig into the jar for the peanut butter.

This was long ago, before peanut butter became the creamy imitation we have today, and the stuff at the bottom of the jar was almost rock-solid. I was just ready to spread the sandwich when, out of the dark, came a very large shadow. Bear. I knew the bear sought food, so I dipped the knife into the jar and scooped out most of the contents, shoved knife and peanut butter at the bear, and went back to the safety of the poker game.

Yes, I know what I did was cruel. Did the other guys believe me? Hell, no. Not until they saw that bear three days later still trying to get his teeth unstuck.

6

Catfishing

One of my earliest recollections of Montana is being drowned by a fish. A small catfish, not the larger ones I later encountered. Actually, for a bullhead (or mud cat) this was a good-sized fish.

When I was six or seven, Ninepipe Reservoir was unfenced and unpolluted. Some great catfish and bass inhabited the lake and they were free to anyone who had a license and a yen. Being dirt poor, we needed any kind of food, so our whole family fished the reservoir.

As long as the water doesn't get too stagnant, catfish make good eating, and even after more than sixty years I often prefer catfish fillets. We often caught our breakfast (and dinner and supper, too) on a Sunday afternoon.

I remember Dad strapping our bamboo poles to the top of the old Chevrolet sedan and driving as near the water as he thought safe. We piled out and each took a bamboo pole and a flour sack for the fish. Dad carried the most valuable supply—a coffee can of large and aggressive angleworms. We didn't have fancy red and white bobbers like the ones I see today. We had corks from wherever we could find them. Must have been a lot of corked bottles then. I know none of the corks we used were from wine bottles, though—Mother was a Methodist. Once in a while we lost a cork, and had to make do with whatever wood chip we could find. Sometimes we chose a chip so big the fish couldn't pull it under water. We lost some good fish that way.

To get to the best fishing, we had to wade through the muck and out into the water. Dad picked a spot thigh-deep to him, but neck-deep to my sister and me. We had to fish near him—he had the worms, remember? When I hooked a fish, I waded back to shore, dragging the fish along onto dry land. Then I had to unhook the thing myself, and get it into that flour sack. Sounds easy, but given a pound of angry fish with three very formidable and poisonous "horns" in his fins, a six or seven-year-old has his hands full. Not only of fish, but of painful punctures from those horns.

I suppose I was about six when I hooked a catfish that must have weighed two pounds. Neck-deep in the water, I couldn't get a toehold, so the fish soon won the ensuing tug-of-war, and dragged me into deeper water. Dad had his own fish on, so he couldn't be bothered to help me until he had taken care of his own chore. By the time he came to help, I was on my way out to sea—or perhaps I should say out to lake. Dad took two steps, grabbed me by the suspenders of my overalls and held me until I coughed up much of the lake, then "landed" the fish and put it safely in my flour sack. You can bet I was proud when Dad announced that I'd caught the biggest fish of the day.

Some people stuff their big fish—but I caught a fish that stuffed our whole family.

The fish planted in Ninepipe were supposed to be kept there by screens at the outflow of the reservoir. Small fish got through, though, and many of the ponds (potholes) had a good stock of fish. As the reservoir was fenced and as the difficulty of getting to the old fishing holes increased, Dad kept an eye and an ear out for good fishing ponds, and carefully cultivated friendships with the farmers who had them. (That's misleading. Dad cultivated friendships with darn near everybody, especially those who were characters or who told a good story. Those with good fishing ponds just happened to be in that group.)

When Dad bought his own farm in 1937, the pond contained sizable catfish, but when he found that a neighboring pond had bigger fish, he left ours, hoping they'd grow into monsters like the ones we found in the reservoir. They never did. Instead, they steadily declined and finally disappeared altogether. Dad blamed the mud turtles for destroying the fish, but the catfish began to disappear in all the potholes with the arrival of the pond weeds, which, we know now, grow in polluted water. I suspect that the pond weeds and their detritus depleted the oxygen so much the fish could not survive.

Later, I fished for catfish in the lakes around Spokane, but none were ever as good as those from Ninepipe. Now, I depend on farm-raised catfish, but they just aren't the same.

The Bumblers

"What the heck do you guys think you're doing?" Dad asked. The way his face twitched, I knew we were in for some serious ribbing.

"Hiding," Dowd answered.

"Who from?"

"Bees."

"Well, that's some disguise you figured out. Reckon nobody'd recognize you. Unless the bees are smarter than you think."

It was all Dad's fault.

When he was a kid in Iowa, he told us, he and his friend Frankie used to go down along the railroad right-of-way in search of bumblebee nests. The railroad embankment drained well and was the only place the heavy Iowa rains didn't drown the bees. When Ernie and Frankie found a nest, they waited until a bee came out, then swatted it with a paddle that they'd made solely for that purpose. It was fun, Dad said, until you missed a bee, then had to dodge that one while trying to swat the next. After you missed several, it was time to cut and run. Somehow, Dowd and I missed that part of the story.

Remember the old Bifbat paddles? I think something of the kind is still around. The Bifbat was a small paddle with a rubber ball attached to it by a length of rubber string. The object, which I never achieved, was to keep batting the ball as it came back from the stretch of the rubber string.

Dowd and I took the ball and rubber string off a couple of Bifbats and set out to hunt bumblebees. (Remember, this was before ecology was invented.) We found the bumblebee nest in the bank of the big ditch that ran through our farm. These were small bees, as bumblebees go, so we supposed they were be easy to fight and their stings were minor. We were wrong on both counts.

When we stirred up the nest, sure enough, the bees came out one by one. I got the first one. But not the second. The escaped bee took one look at the situation, decided who was the enemy, and came right for me. I missed the third bee, too, then the fourth, fifth and probably the fifteenth. Dowd was wiser than I and had distanced himself from the action as soon as I missed that second bee.

We dived into the ditch, but when we came up to breathe, we found the air aswarm with angry bumblebees. Dowd grabbed some clay mud from the bottom and covered his face, the only part he held above water. The mud discouraged the bees, so I followed his example. Soon we managed to coat our heads and hands and arms heavily with clay mud so we could sit up in the ditch. The bees swarmed around us for a while; then, one by one, they went home to assess the damage and go about their daily routine. About that time, Dad found us.

"Now, what bees are you hiding from?"

"Bumblebees."

"How come you have to hide from them? How'd you stir them up?"

"Well, you told us about batting bees when you were a kid, and we thought we'd try it. I got the first one, but they were too fast for me."

Dad's face got redder under his normal red tan.

"I don't suppose you understand that we need the bumblebees to fertilize the alfalfa seed. Honeybees can't get the blooms open, but bumblebees can. I don't want you bothering bumblebees again."

The last order was unnecessary. We had both taken vows (underwater, to be sure) never even to get *close* to a bumblebee nest in the immediate or distant future.

This story could have ended here, had not the bees come back about then. Dad was highly allergic to bee stings, so when they came toward him, he joined us in the water. Knowing his weakness, we went to work with the mud and soon had him well protected.

All would have been well, had not H.B.[1] come wandering along the ditch bank. He was smoking his pipe, and the bees wanted no part of the smoke from the rich tobacco he used. They took one sniff and decided they had business elsewhere. When he saw us sitting in the water, fully clothed and thoroughly encased in mud, H.B. started to chuckle, then guffaw, and finally he sat down on the bank too weak to laugh.

"Y'all tryin' a new beauty treatment there? If y'are, it ain't workin'," he managed to get out.

We looked around at each other and had to agree with him. It wasn't real easy to laugh, though, with that clay mud caked on our faces.

---

[1]See "H.B.", *Building Character:Tales from Montana (And Other Damn Lies)* page 89.

The Man Eaters

A few years ago, I asked a dermatologist about a couple of wart-like growths that become large as a pinhead, at which time I remove them with my fingernail. They always come back, though. When I told him this, he asked if I had been exposed to cyanide when I was young. I told him no, but when "cyanide" jogged my memory, some events came forth that I had almost forgotten.

When I was eight or nine years old, our house became infested with bedbugs. These varmints chew a line of holes along your body, and leave you itching for days. Mother said the house sparrows brought the bedbugs in when they nested under the eaves, but I suspect we picked them up when we stayed overnight with some not too sanitary neighbors. Dad fumigated the house with cyanide gas, and even though he left the house to air for a day or so we still found spots where the unmistakable odor of cyanide remained. Got rid of those man-eaters, though.

We used cyanide gas on gophers, too. I personally dumped a bit of cyanide crystals, followed by a half cup of water, into gopher holes. As soon as the water hit the crystals, we could smell the gas, and we had to seal the hole up quickly. So, yes, doctor, I was exposed to cyanide— many times.

Used to be that the Mission Valley was swarming with mosquitoes. The irrigation reservoirs and the many potholes were ideal breeding grounds and the mosquitoes rose in swarms. They weren't as big as the Louisiana mosquitoes who have been known to carry off a man's mule and then pitch horseshoes (muleshoes?) to see which one got the rider. No. Montana mosquitoes were smaller, but if there was a contest for total weight per square mile, they'd have made those Louisiana skeeters look at their hole card.

Montana mosquitoes may be small, but they have bills that must be eighteen inches long. Maybe they coil them up in their bodies—when they bite, you know you've been *bitten*.

The mosquitoes usually attacked just after sundown. They came out in clouds that darkened the sky, and made us use bandannas for protection because, as Dad often said, they got into your eyes and your ears and into your mouth when you started to cuss them. Eventually, those of us who lived on farms and couldn't avoid being bitten developed some kind of immunity to (or at least tolerance of) their bites. Until recently, a single mosquito bite swelled on me each year, restoring my immunity so my body ignored subsequent bites. Lately, though, more and more bites swell. I guess I'm not getting enough toxin from that first bite to inoculate me.

Wood ticks were another matter. Rocky Mountain Spotted Fever was deadly back in the 1930s and those of us who went into the timber at certain times of the year (virtually everybody, that is) were careful to de-tick one another. This required an examination of the entire body, especially any area with hair. I went picnicking in the woods many times and with many different girls, and each time, as a gentleman should, I offered to de-tick the lady. Somehow, she always seemed willing to wait until she got home.

Once a tick became embedded, volunteers with cures were as numerous as those who appear when someone has the hiccups. One suggestion was to hold a burning cigarette close to the tick. I tried that—got a fried wood tick and a big blister. A common suggestion was to wash the tick with kerosene. I never had much success with that, either. Lately, one is told to cover the tick with petroleum jelly so it can't breathe, and it will let go. Either the tick I tried that with could hold its breath for a long time, or it smothered. I use other methods to rid myself on the darn things now.

The most effective solution I've heard is this: take hold of the tick with tweezers and pull *gently* until the tick lets go. I did something similar when I was in the fourth grade and had an itchy knot the size of a cherry pit in my hair. I kept poking at it until it got up and walked away. That's when I realized my knot was a wood tick full of blood.

Alas, I don't get out in the woods as much as I used to. I haven't had a tick on me for—let's see now—two, no, three months.

Open Skylight?

Old Gabriel Smee
Lives up in a tree
With possums and squirrels and birds.
When Gabriel speaks
Of how his tree leaks
He uses all four-letter words.

15

Animal Bites

Nowadays, when someone's bitten by any kind of animal, that animal is quarantined and examined to make sure it isn't rabid, else the bitee has to have rabies shots. If that mind-set had been around when I was a kid, I'd have kept my parents broke with the doctor bills. Come to think of it, that isn't true—they were broke already.

I've been bitten by about any kind of animal you can find on a farm. One of my earliest recollections is of a mouse bite. Our resident cat had caught a mouse and, not being hungry at the moment, was playing with the poor thing; letting it run, then catching it, bringing it back and letting it run again. Sometimes cats act almost human.

I thought to save the poor mousey, so I beat the cat to it and picked it up by the tail. The mouse, to show its gratitude, turned around, climbed up its tail, and bit me. Those sharp little teeth cut all the way through my five-year-old finger. Of course, I jerked back, throwing the mouse into some tall grass, and started to yell. The cat looked at me in disgust and walked away, her tail jerking from side to side. With my finger dripping blood, I ran to Mother for comfort.

"Now, what?" she asked.

"The m-m-m..." I realized that if I told what really happened, it would cause quite an uproar, so I changed my story. "I c-c-cut myself on the b-b-barb wire." Since that happened once or twice a week anyway, I knew it wouldn't upset Mother. It didn't. She bandaged me with carbolated Vaseline and sent me out to get into more trouble.

Hunting gophers with a .22 led to another animal bite. Most of the time when I shot a gopher, the shot was fatal or else the dog finished the gopher off. Only rarely did a wounded gopher escape down a hole. My father taught me to put any a seriously wounded animal, be it tame or wild, out of its misery, so when I wounded a gopher and it could be heard whistling just inside its hole, I donned my leather glove for protection and reached down to pull the animal out for my dog to finish. The gopher didn't know I was doing it a favor, nor that the glove was supposed to protect my hand. It bit right through the glove and my finger. It didn't let go quickly enough, though, so when I jerked my hand back reflexively, I threw the gopher twenty feet away. Since I was yelling and cursing (I probably said something like *darn it!*), my dog took up my defense and thoroughly killed the miscreant gopher.

I have only been bitten twice by dogs other than my own. Both times were my own fault. Once, I assumed it safe to pet a dog just because it belonged to a good friend. The other time, I assumed the dog's chain wasn't long enough to let it reach the sidewalk. That's the trouble with assumptions. They bite.

My own little bulldog gave me the worst bite and the only attractive dog-bite scar I own. Until I learned better, I used to hold a stick and get her to jump for it. I held it high and she gathered herself and jumped until I either lowered it, or she finally caught it. One day, she caught the stick but caught my finger too. Of course I screamed and cussed (*darn it!* again) and when she realized she'd hurt me, she was so contrite I couldn't help stopping to comfort her. With a bloody hand, at that.

Everybody who plays roughly with a cat will be bitten sometimes. Most often it's a playful bite that won't break the skin—but let that playful cat be cornered or hurt or scared, look out. When my favorite cat—a gentle, loving thing—followed a mouse between hay bales in the barn and got stuck, she panicked and squalled for help. When I pulled her out, she turned on me and bit right through that same old wounded finger. She was not contrite like the dog. She held a grudge for weeks—blaming me, I suppose, for the predicament she had gotten herself into.

I was bitten by a cow. Well, not actually by a cow—by a calf. Calves don't need upper front teeth, so they don't have them. Once we had a new bull calf that needed to be weaned from his mother and taught to drink from a bucket. We usually weaned a calf right away because if you wait a week or so, a bull calf can butt surprisingly hard. I made the mistake of dreading the job too long, so the little rascal was ten days old before I began his training.

Sucking milk up from a bucket is not the normal way for a calf to drink, and he let me know it. To teach him, I straddled the little beggar, grabbed his nose with one hand, curled a middle finger down and into his mouth, and when he started to suck the finger, forced his head down into the bucket. As he began to get milk sucking on the finger, I moved the finger out.

The first few times, the calf responded with a butt. Now, remember that finger curled down into his mouth, and his lower teeth (sharp ones, you can bet) were on the tender skin on the back of my finger. He bit! And the damage done to the in-the-mouth finger was enough to make me say, "Oh, for pity's sake!" For the week or so it took the calf to catch on to drinking from a pail, my finger was skinned raw.

Then there was the horse. Our horses on the farm were placid, friendly animals. Oh, if they hadn't worked for a while, they sometimes played hard-to-get with us when we went to catch them up. When I walked out to the pasture with the bridles, they ran away as if I were a

18

stranger. When I finally got them into a corner of the pasture, they pretended to be submissive, then broke and ran past me to the farthest fence, laughing at me all the way. After a few repeats of their little joke, it became apparent to them that my temper was fast approaching meltdown, so they calmed down and allowed me to walk right up and put the bridles on.

Dowd's pony was not like that. He wasn't a wild horse, but he had a mean streak that showed up most often with someone who didn't know him well.

When Dowd offered me a ride, I swung up into the saddle, but found the stirrups were too long for me. Dowd offered to adjust them, and went to work on the left stirrup. The horse reached around for the other stirrup and managed to clamp his teeth onto the toe of my right boot. He was reluctant to let go, but with his head around like that, he could do little but turn in a tight circle. I wanted to get off, but I would have had to leave one foot there, and that didn't seem like a good idea. Screaming more in anger than in pain, I tried to beat him off with the reins as we spun merrily around.

Dowd wasn't much help, rolling around on the ground the way he was. The horse had done the same to him, and for someone else to get caught seemed hilariously funny to him. After what seemed like an hour or two, the horse must have gotten a crick in his neck, because he let go, and stood absolutely still while we adjusted the stirrups. I expected him to try to buck then; but no, he was docile as a lamb, and hardly any fun to ride at all.

Only once did I experience an animal bite that resulted in illness, and even then I was only indisposed for a few days. It happened when Dowd, Murdie and I set out to go camping with Elroy Blurch. Elroy's family moved away from Charlo clear up near the Canadian border, and

19

a year or so later, Elroy wrote that he missed us and wished we'd come visit him. He bragged about the scenery and the wildlife in the area, said that both far outshone that of the lower Flathead Valley. Forgetting that Elroy was a walking disaster area, we planned a visit, aiming all the while to camp out and fish.

Elroy exaggerated about the scenery. As we had suspected, the mountains were no higher nor more rugged than the Mission Mountains. He was, however, right about the wildlife. Life in the saloon near his house was about as wild any I've ever seen. But we hadn't come for that kind of entertainment. We talked Elroy into leading us to a remarkably productive fishing lake a few miles into the wilderness.

The weather turned cold as soon as we got settled in our fishing camp. We toughed it out until the morning of the third day. By then I wore all the clothes I had brought with me. I wore long underwear, a flannel shirt, a sweater and my standard denim jacket and still was shivering. After breaking up the ice along the lake shore to get water for coffee, we agreed to call off the trip and leave the fish for another day.

Tramping along the trail toward town warmed us a bit, until an unearthly howl froze our goose pimples in the upright position. On the trail ahead of us appeared what, at first, we thought must be a big dog, but its size and the color of its eyes told us otherwise. It was a wolf. Not only that, the foam around its jaws told us more.

"Mad dog, uh, wolf!" Dowd gasped from his perch twenty feet up a pine tree.

"Run, Chicken, run," Murdie called from the top branches of a cottonwood. I still wonder how they got so high when I was still spinning my feet, trying to get traction. The wolf sprang at me.

I didn't have time for even my short life to flash before my eyes. Instinctively, I stuck out my arm, surprising the wolf, who overshot his mark and found my hand in his mouth. Without thinking, I rammed my hand in as far as I could, then grabbed whatever I could. I don't know the medical term for what I had hold of, but I'd call it the base of his tongue. The wolf gagged, and tried to pull free. I knew if he did, I was in for it, so I held on as hard as I could. My jacket protected my arm from his fangs for a trice, but the material soon gave way and he began slicing away at my arm. All I could do was keep him from getting my hand and arm into those big, crunching molars. I don't know how long it took—it seemed like hours to me—but my hand was strangling him, and eventually he weakened and finally he slumped down and quit altogether. When all was quiet, my friends climbed down and found me lying there with a dead wolf at the end of my arm, so tired I had gone to sleep. Of course they thought I was dead, but when I woke up and cussed them for leaving me, they peeled off the wolf, gagging when they saw all the puncture wounds on my arm. They refused to touch them for fear of being exposed to rabies themselves. When I got my wits about me, I asked Dowd to get the package of Peerless tobacco I'd sneaked into my pack. He hesitated, but when I started to get up, he tossed the package to me and backed away. I took a big wad and chewed until I had enough spit and tobacco to make a poultice for the bites. My friends refused to touch the rabid wolf again, let alone skin it, and I only had one usable hand, so we let it lie.

For the next few days, I was laid up in bed, horribly sick. Rabies? Hell, no. Rabies virus can't abide Peerless tobacco. Neither can I. I can handle Copenhagen, but I never could stomach that Peerless. Gives me a bad case of the flu every time.

Spoiled Brat

Harold wasn't aware of it, but he performed a miracle that summer. He united a nine-year-old boy with his eleven-year-old sister.

In 1935, my cousin Evelyn came to Montana with her husband and her three-year-old boy, Harold. Evelyn was fourteen or fifteen years older than my sister Ruth and I, and was one of Mother's favorite nieces, perhaps because she had helped Mother cope when Ruth and I were small children.

The time was the depths of the Depression, and I think the family came to sponge off anyone they could. The husband was a city boy and wasn't worth much as a farm hand, but Dad put up with him for the sake of peace in the family, and because their small family had a good chance of starving without some help.

Putting it as kindly as I can: Harold was a spoiled brat. Both my mother and Evelyn worked hard at spoiling him, and Ruth and I resented it mightily. Of course, we had no experience with younger children in the house, and cutesy expressions of a child of that age were lost on us.

I remember that Harold was wont to say, when ordered to do something, "I suppose I have to," in a resigned tone. One of Mother's pet expressions was, "Well, excuse me for living!" And when Harold responded, "I suppose I have to," Ruth and I were aghast at the "sass." If I had said that, I'd have been back-handed across the room. but Harold said it, and Mother and Evelyn thought it was too cute for words.

Each time Harold was given preference because of his age, Ruth and I magnified it into a gross insult. I remember clearly once when I was playing with my cat—*my* cat—Harold, in the manner of any spoiled three-year-old, claimed priority. I refused to give him the cat, and Harold prepared a tantrum. Evelyn came over, and with her toe, pushed me aside, and said, "Let Harold have the kitty." By the time I discussed the event with Ruth, it became *Evelyn kicked me out of the way.*

Ruth and I were stuck trying to decide what to do. Harold followed us everywhere and interfered with whatever we were doing. Every day, while Harold took a nap, we plotted and planned all manner of spiteful actions, none of which seemed practicable. We couldn't lure him into the ditch to drown him—any ditch we were allowed near was too shallow to do much harm. We considered losing Harold in the swamp—but that plan, too, had a flaw. We were afraid to go into the swamp ourselves, fearing the monsters that might be there and fearing *we* might get lost.

I don't remember how long Evelyn and her family lived with us—probably only a few months—but it was 'way too many years as far as Ruth and I were concerned. To this day, I have an aversion to the name Harold. And even though I knew where Harold was twenty years or so ago, I didn't look him up. Wish I had. One of us might have changed.

But that time with Harold as a mutual enemy made Ruth and me friends for a while, although we were never again that close until after she married and had children.

When I think back, I sometimes wonder if some of my own children might have made the same type of bonding because of the irritating action of younger siblings. There was certainly enough of *that* to go around.

The Slide

Entertainment was so hard to come by during the not-so-Great Depression that we improvised or "made do" however we could. I don't think most children nowadays understand the "make do or do without" mentality that influenced our growing up.

A large feeder irrigation ditch ran above the edge of a pothole near our grade school. The ditch was not of much interest except in summer, when it served as a swimming hole in which to get caught bare naked[2], or in the winter, when the resulting embankment provided us with an ice slide long enough to be entertaining. The slide down the bank ended abruptly at a forest of cattails at the edge of the pond. We might have cut the cattails and extended the run, but the pothole was rumored to be infinitely deep and to have springs that caused holes in the ice. Our parents forbade us to venture out onto it, although once in a while one of the older boys, perhaps with a death wish, tried the ice. No one, to my knowledge, ever fell through. Sometime in the last sixty years, the town filled the "infinitely deep" pond and built a baseball field over it.

In good weather (temperature below 20°) the slide was *the* place to go at recess. We packed the snow down by tramping up and down the hill until it was too slick to stand on. If there wasn't enough snow to make a good slide, or if we wore the snow off by too much use, we boys used to break the ice in the ditch and carry water from the ditch and pour it on the slide. We did this before school in the morning, whenever we had any time. At home, the *work* of carrying two buckets of water ten yards over level

---

[2]See "The Bare Necessities," *More Montana: Tall Tales, Damn Lies and Otherwise* page 22.

ground was sure to tire us to exhaustion. In those early mornings, the *fun* of carrying dozens of bucketfuls up the ditch bank tired us not at all.

To enhance our macho image, we boys slid down the ice path standing. After sliding down facing downhill a time or two, I took my aching behind aside and learned to slide down sideways. At least one had a chance of reaching the bottom without serious damage to his person—and ego. Smaller children standing near the bottom were sometimes scattered like bowling pins, but they should have known the hazards.

Few of us brought sleds to school, and those who did found the sleds usurped by older and bigger boys. Two guys named Wayne and Howie always took the best sleds. Our need for toys was met by a miserly old man who lived near the school yard. Mr. Buford collected old iron— machinery and parts, mostly. For our slide we "borrowed" from his piles of iron anything that might keep our little behinds off the ice. An old shovel without a handle worked well, as did a single disk from a disk-harrow. One guy tried a large tin can, almost a barrel. He lived.

The slide could be dangerous in more ways than one. The nearest I came to catastrophe came about because I had discovered an especially large and smooth disk in Mr. Buford's collection. I dragged it over to the slide and started down. Once moving, I was in free fall, and gaining speed all the way. I forgot to notice that Wayne and Howie were standing halfway down the slide. My onrushing vehicle swept them off their feet, and their cries for vengeance followed me down the hill. When my journey ended at the cattails, I kept going, running through the reeds out onto the dangerous ice. The ice creaked underneath me, but I thought drowning in icy water would be a less painful death than that promised me by Wayne and Howie. When the bell rang for the end of recess, my enemies slowly retreated and I returned to shore, cold and chastened. My chariot was gone, to show up later under the control (and bottoms) of Wayne and Howie.

When the weather warmed, we could no longer maintain the slide. The ice wouldn't keep and the remaining snow became wet and heavy, just right for making snowballs and snow forts. We went on to other sports—snowball wars, and most fun of all, throwing snowballs at the girls' outhouse.

To Becky
December 1997

I happen to know you like the snow
And I know you'd have loved last night.
The clouds hung low, reflecting the glow
Of the city's every light.

Like powder puffs that winter stuff's
On every branch and tree.
A Christmas scene is what I mean.
It's really a sight to see.

I know we'll miss displays like this
In the holiday season this year.
But better yet is the joy we'll get
When our loving family's near.

Starstruck

Conventional wisdom says a cow can't kick backward. Well, it's true a cow can't kick like a horse, but sometimes she can kick backward far enough to be dangerous. One kicked me far enough to more than endanger me: she embarrassed hell out of me.

Most of the time, the few milch cows we kept were pets. You could walk among them as they grazed and they'd never miss a bite. You'd never expect pets like them to be dangerous.

Cows have personalities as different as their color and markings. In the spring of 1939, we had three milch cows, Gretchen, Bess and Star. Old Gretchen (all our cows received the appellation "old" as soon as they bore calves) was phlegmatic and so tame she was hard to drive around. Sometimes I had to push her.

Old Bess was senior in the pecking order, and a tyrant to the other cows, but such a pet she'd sometimes come over and nuzzle up to me to get me to scratch her head, and that, too, could be dangerous. Once she nuzzled me along a stretch of barb wire fence, causing serious scratches to my self respect. Sometimes when I brought the cows home from the far pasture, I'd ride one. Old Star was my favorite cow to ride because she'd trot right along, and her swinging gait made for an easy ride.

Star was cooperative and willing to let me ride, but she didn't like surprises. At least one hump in my back came about after I played Buck Jones and jumped astraddle her from the barn roof. Star played bronco and bucked me higher than most horses could. After I got my head out of the muck in the barn lot, I washed up and never told my parents that I'd hurt my back really bad. In their sympathy, they'd have warmed my britches for treating the cow that way.

One night, I had milked old Bess, and had only Star to milk before I could go to the house and listen to Fibber McGee on the radio. I didn't mean to surprise Star this time, but she must have been asleep or something. As I was about to sit down, she kicked the stool and me deftly across the floor. The stool bounced off the wall but I, being less rigid, didn't go so far. I wound up in the gutter. Being rather slight (skinny) I fit into the gutter quite well. I'll pause now for the snide remarks about my current figure.

For those of you who are unfamiliar with the barn of yesteryear, I guess I need to describe the situation. At the time, we milked two cows. Old Gretchen was dry, but, being a cow of habit, she came in with the milkers into our four-stanchion barn. The cows were so tame that half the time I didn't bother to lock the stanchions. In fact, I sometimes had to crawl into the manger and push the cows' heads out to get them to leave the barn. If you saw the depth of the mud in the feedlot outside, you'd understand their reluctance. The wooden floor of the barn was long enough for the cows to stand comfortably, and behind them ran a gutter. At the time of this incident, the cows were on fresh grass. Anyone who's been on a farm knows what the gutter was like.

Even though I was a skinny hundred pounds or so, I fit tightly in the gutter. To my horror, I fell directly behind Old Star, who was laying for me. When I raised my head, a hoof came whistling by my face, missing my chin by a whisker, of which said chin bore none. I tried again, and so did Star.

I had three choices. I could call for Dad, I could wait for him to find me, or I could move along the gutter out of Star's reach.

Two considerations kept me from yelling for Dad. The cows, standing unfastened in the stanchions, might panic and step all over me on their way out of the barn. Also, chances of Dad hearing me were poor, and if he found me in this position, it was an even bet he'd laugh himself to death, and if he didn't, H.B. might when Dad told him the story, what with the embellishments Dad was bound to put in. No, calling out wouldn't do.

I supposed I could wait for Dad to find me. He'd come looking for me to raise hell with me for taking so long with the milking, and when he found me—well, the same result as if I'd called him. And if I waited, sooner or later Star might decide to relieve herself, and looking up, I could see that my face was strategically in a very poor position.

I had to move, and that was not easy. The trough fit snugly around me, and Star stood watchfuly over me. Also, the contents of the gutter left little friction to move me about. I finally managed to get a boot out so I could hook a bit of the floor and push myself along the gutter. About a quarter inch. I tried again. Another quarter inch. On the third try, I found a flaw in the floor and managed an inch and a half. Bit by bit, I slid myself along the gutter. I needed to get my whole upper torso out of Star's reach before I tried to get out. But by the time I had done that, I was looking up into Gretchen's arsenal, so to speak.

I eased myself to a sitting position. Gretchen had never kicked—but for all I knew, she might have been taking lessons from Star. I scrambled out of the gutter and stood there shivering, wet and cold. I thought of beating Star to death with the milk stool. I thought of giving the milking up as a bad job and going back to the house to clean up. Honor bound, and more afraid of Dad's derision than his anger, I wiped my hands on Old Star's back and sat down and milked the damn cow, although "damn" is the mildest and cleanest of the words I used to describe her as I sat there.

When I got to the house, Dad's first reaction was surprise, and it must have been about a tenth of a second before he caught on.

"What happened to you?" he asked, feigning concern, though the corners of his mouth were twitching.

"Nothing!"

"Well is cow manure—" he didn't say manure. "Is cow manure the new rage in beauty treatments?"

I nearly threw the bucket of milk over him, but milk was worth money and the loss just wasn't worth it.

When I told him that Star had kicked me into the gutter, he just nodded, but I could tell he was snickering already.

"Come over by the well," he said.

"Not by the well!" Mother shouted out the back door. "Out by the driveway." A lot of sympathy I got. I moved out into the back yard.

While Dad threw bucket after bucket of icy well water over me and I peeled away each layer of drenched clothing, he wormed the details out of me. By the time I was washed Dad was laughing so hard he could hardly aim the bucket, but I was cooled off, both in body and temper.

Of course, Dad could hardly wait to tell H.B. Neither of them laughed as hard as I had feared. I have a hard time laughing about it at all, even now.

The Teamster

As the horses sloshed into the mire, it was apparent that the mud was deeper than the old man expected. Halfway through the muddy patch, the horses slipped and stumbled, and the wagon slowed and finally stopped. The team struggled for a bit, trying to find footing, then gave up, blowing and shifting in their harness, undecided.

Most teamsters, the boy knew, turned the air blue (perhaps purple) at this sort of development. Atop the loaded wagon the old man surveyed the situation and spoke only one word.

"DRAT."

A rifle shot would not have been as crisp. The boy was sure the surrounding trees shook as the echoes paraded back from the hills.

As one, the horses jerked up their heads, eyes rolling, before settling against their collars. With super-equine effort, they moved the wagon, so slowly it was hardly noticeable at first, then faster, and soon they pulled it to solid ground, where they stopped, trembling, without command. The old man wrapped the reins and took out his pipe.

"Thanks, boys," he said.

The boy had come with his grandfather only after long negotiations with his mother before she gave her final reluctant acquiescence. For him it was a holiday, and the grandfather was glad of his company, assuring him that he'd be of great help. While the old man loaded the logs on the wagon, the boy darted about, trying to be helpful, performing the simple tasks his grandfather commanded. Patiently, his grandfather taught him about log chains and how to hook them, and how to use a peavey. He even let the boy drive the horses for simple tasks. Once the

31

wagon was loaded, the boy felt free to wander a bit, and he walked behind the wagon until it became mired.

The track wound among the trees on the way to the main road. Experience with the first mudhole made the old man cautious, so before he reached a puddle, he halted the team to examine the prospects. Sometimes he urged the horses on through, but at some of the deeper holes he drove carefully alongside the deep, permanent ruts. The boy, dawdling along behind, dropped back, but caught up with the wagon at each mudhole. The old man stopped the team before an extra-deep mudhole and waited for the boy to come up.

"You best get ready to ride," the old man said. "This is near the last hole I'll have to stop for. It'll be downhill most of the way to the road, and you won't be able to keep up. I'm gonna drive around this one, and then I want you up here with me."

The boy nodded. He was beginning to tire anyway and wanted a chance to rest, although the evening air of late March was chilly and he knew he'd be cold on the wagon.

The grandfather eased the wagon around the mudhole, left wheels making a new trail and right wheels hanging on the frozen ground at the edge of the rut. Suddenly, a rear wheel slid sideways into the deep rut, and the top-heavy load teetered for an instant, then rolled ponderously sideways. The old man jumped, but not far enough. One of the rolling logs caught his legs, pinning him to the ground.

The boy watched horrified. Had he just watched his grandpa die? The horses stopped, and when the logs settled down, the boy ran to his grandfather. The old man was pale under his perpetual tan, and he gritted his teeth in pain.

"Grandpa?" the boy asked hesitantly.

The old man turned to him and grated out, "I'm all right." A lie, the boy knew.

"What'll I do, Grandpa?" The boy thought of running the five miles home for help. Lots of good that would do. What could his mother and grandmother do?

The old man took some deep breaths and spoke slowly. "You'll have to get me loose. Not time to get help. Ground's frozen. I'd die."

The words chilled the boy to the coldness of the ground. "What can I do?"

"See can you lift the end of the log."

The boy strained at the log, but couldn't budge it.

"Maybe if I get the peavey I can roll the log off."

"NO!" The old man's voice was sharp. "Don't roll it. I don't think I'm hurt too bad yet. There's brush under me for a cushion. But if you roll this thing it will go over my foot. You gotta lift it."

Lift it? The boy's heart sank. He'd tried, but the log was just too heavy.

"See can you find the skid poles I used to load the wagon." These were shorter, smaller logs.

The boy ran to the spilled load and found the poles near the top. He worked one loose and dragged it back to his grandfather.

"Can you work it under the log and prize it up?"

The boy could barely move the pole, but he tried several places and finally found one where the pole slid under. He lifted on the end of the lever, but could not move the log.

"Get the team," his grandfather ordered. The boy struggled with the neck yoke and the doubletree, but finally unhitched the patient horses from the wagon and drove them toward the old man. He stopped when the horses were near the man's head. The nearest horse put in

33

head down to the man's face and smelled. The man raised his hand and rubbed the muzzle.

"You boys are gonna get me out of this," he said. To the boy, he said, "I been studying what to do. You get the log chain over here."

The boy ran to get the chain from the wagon. It was so heavy he could barely carry all of it without dragging. He dropped it near his grandfather. The old man rose on his elbows.

"Now, you do just what I tell you. Don't hurry, understand? Run the chain under the end of that prize pole. That's it. Now hook it up tight so it won't slip. Now go get the other skid pole." The old man lay back to rest. The boy needed rest, too, but he wanted to do whatever needed to be done to free his grandfather. He ran to the load, found the pole, worked it loose and dragged it to the old man.

"Now, haul the chain over that pile of logs there, so it's higher that the one on me. There, that's it. Now take the team over there and hitch to the chain but first, listen. When they pull on the pry log, they can't move far, or they'll make it roll. Now hitch them, then go talk to them like I taught you."

The boy drove the team around and made the hitch, then walked to the horses' heads. "Easy, boys," he said, as his grandfather had taught him. He found comfort in their friendly nuzzling.

"Tighten up the chain, but don't pull yet," came the order. "Easy, boys." The horses laid their ears back at the sound of the old man's voice and eased against the traces. When the chain was tight, the boy called, "Whoa." The horses stopped, with the chain nearly taut.

"STEP," the old man called.

34

As one, the horses moved one step. Holding the reins, the boy felt helpless. He wasn't doing anything. The man and the horses were doing this as one. The chain tightened, but the pole did not move. The boy looked anxiously at his grandfather.

"STEP," the old man spoke again. This time the pry pole moved several inches.

"Put that other skid pole under the log next to me," the old man said. The boy did as he was told.

"STEP."

The log raised a few more inches.

"Move this pole to that high point there. No, not there, over there."

The boy hastened to obey, but the pole was heavy and he was clumsy with it. When the log was in place, the old man nodded.

"Take the reins, and slack the chain."

"But the log..."

"Do what I say." For the first time this day, the grandfather spoke sharply to him.

The boy picked up the reins, looked once at his grandfather.

"Back," he said, pulling gently on the reins.

The horses backed off one step. The big log settled back onto the skid poles, but free of the old man's leg.

"Now take that chain and hook it around the log at that end, there, like I taught you. Bring the horses around so they'll be pulling the log straight."

The boy repositioned the team and the chain as directed.

"Now, boy, go get the peavey and set it in the log."

The peavey, too, was almost all the boy could handle, but he managed to do as he was told.

"Try not to let the log roll, all right?"

The boy wondered if he could hold the log, but knew he had to try. The old man spoke to the team again.

"Step," he said softly. The team took one step. The log didn't move.

"Step." The log moved a few inches. The boy leaned against the peavey as the log tried to roll.

"Step." Another few inches.

"Step." The space between man and log was greater now. "Easy boys. Giddap." The team moved slowly away. When the log cleared the old man's body, he called, "Whoa." The team stopped as if against a wall.

The old man struggled to rise, but cried out in pain.

"Boy, take the team around to the far side of the wagon, hook that chain on, and right the wagon. You can do it. I know you can."

Cheered by his success with the log, the boy hurried the team around as told. Compared to moving the log, righting the wagon was easy.

"Good boy," the old man called. "Hitch 'em up."

When the horses were once again hitched to the wagon, the old man called the boy over.

"You gotta help me up. Don't look so scared. You can do it."

It seemed to take hours of agonized straining, but the boy and the old man finally were on the wagon bed.

"Take us home, boy. Take us home."

Scared but proud, the boy shook the lines and, straight-backed, drove the wagon down the rutted trail to the main road. Each time the wagon jounced and his grandfather winced, the boy flinched inwardly. The main road was smoother, and the grandfather seemed to sleep. He roused when they made the turn into the farm lane. The boy brought the wagon as close to the house as he could. By the time he stopped, his mother was running toward him.

"What are your doing driving those horses?" She sounded worried and angry. "Where's your Grandpa?"

The grandfather rose on his elbows.

"Leave the boy be. He handled those horses nigh as well as I can. He's the best teamster you ever seen."

Then he fainted.

"Shivaree"

The charivari was a common custom in the not-so-old days. Friends and neighbors gathered at the newlyweds' home, beat on pans and shovels and generally made a racket. The bridegroom was supposed to come out and serve refreshments to everyone.

Old Ansel was tighter than the bark on a tree, and everyone was surprised when he got married, but they held a charivari anyway. Trouble was, Ansel and his bride hid out, and refused to treat the crowd. Angry at the breach of etiquette, the crowd entered the house, poured all the flavoring extracts together, poured pepper in all the cracks of the wood stove, stopped up the chimney with newspapers, and put the buggy on the roof.

I'll bet some of my more mature readers have some even better "shivaree" stories. If so, I'd like to hear them.

Trapped

When we moved to Montana, we were cut off from our relatives by over a thousand miles of mostly gravel roads. I didn't know any of those folks well enough to be fond of them, but my parents missed them badly. To keep up the ties, we made two trips to our roots in Iowa when I was a boy. One trip, in 1934, I remember because that was the only time I can recall seeing my Grandma Hoskins. I suspect we made the trip that year because Grandma was ailing. She died before we made the second trip in 1937.

Nineteen thirty-six was the year Dad made some money; enough to put down payments on a farm and on a Ford pickup. Dad built a sort of primitive camper shell, with a wooden frame and canvas forming the top and walls. My sister and I rode in the back of the pickup; and, unless it was raining, we rolled the walls of our little house up so we could see the countryside in some aspect other than receding.

We visited around Iowa, seeing various aunts and uncles, many of whom I've forgotten completely. One aunt and uncle and their children, our cousins, are indelibly stamped in my mind. On the way to their farm, Dad stopped and bought a pile of fifteen small watermelons. I think he paid a *whole dollar*. Dad's sister fed us well and we all—uncle, aunt, cousins and ourselves—had an all-you-can-eat-and-more watermelon feed.

Watermelon (if you haven't noticed) is a diuretic. During the night, I got up to respond to the call of nature (and watermelon) and almost panicked. Not knowing where the chamber pot (if there was one) was kept, and, at eleven years old, too embarrassed to wake a cousin for directions, I set out looking for a place to relieve myself. The open upstairs window provided my first hope. I let fly out the window and was aghast to hear the results rattling on a washtub hung below on the side of the house. What if someone heard? What would they think of me? I managed to pinch off, and, desperate now, felt my way to the stairs and through the house to the back door. I stumbled off the porch and made a run for the outhouse. Dark as it was, I sat down and just then three monstrous dogs appeared, baying at me through the open door. They must have wondered who this stranger was, sneaking into that important building in the middle of the night. I slammed the door, but the dogs kept up their barking.

Many thoughts went through my panicky mind. What if I had to stay here all night? How could I sleep? The odor wasn't too bad, but there was no place to lay my head. And what if someone came out and found me trapped?

The worst of my fears came true. Roused by the racket the dogs made, a someone came out to shush them. When they quieted, I peeked out the door and my self-esteem dropped to zero. It was a girl cousin. There was nothing to do but shuffle past her, head down, into the house. I sneaked a peek back outside, only to see her duck into the facilities.

Next morning I dreaded going down to breakfast, expecting a razzing about my midnight adventures. No one said a word, although everyone must have been wakened by the uproar the dogs made. My cousin did wink at me, though.

The Ultimate Comfort Station

My friends have given me several books relating to outhouses. All of the books lament the passing of that good old structure, but, although I enjoy the nostalgia of the books, the demise of the outhouse brings only one comment from me: "Thank God!"

Mrs. Lynch didn't belong on a hardscrabble farm in Montana. She was artistically inclined and used to the better things in life. These things she told the other ladies in our area. Often. Mother liked her anyway and shrugged off her lamentations, saying she just liked to put on airs.

Her artistic inclinations showed up in unusual places, the most visible being that necessary little adjunct, her biffy. Mrs. Lynch had a fully appointed outhouse. She had installed rugs, wallpaper, and framed pictures, and had covered the bench with velour. The round cover for the hole—a smoothed and padded oval in itself—was covered with gathered velvet with a silk rose attached at the center. A plaque on the wall further showed Mrs. Lynch's artistic leanings:

> Whoever comes to this here place
> Night or day in any case
> We wish you heartily in the main
> Good delivery without pain.
> But when you're through please do not tarry
> Remember others may be in a hurry.

Not very good poetry, maybe, but better reading than the Sears Roebuck catalog. Personally, I was never at ease in that much comfort—at the Lynch place, I used the barn.

Old Zeke

There would have been no trouble if Millie had not been along. (Yup. Just like a man. Blame it on the woman.)

Dad and Bill Ward planned a trip to the foothills to scout some trees to cut for firewood on the land owned by Peter Lozeau. Pete's son Joe was a school friend of mine and I begged to go along. I would not have been allowed to go had not Millie Ward cajoled her father into letting her go. Dad said I could be company for Millie, though what company an eight-year-old girl could be to a nine-year-old boy was beyond me at the time.

Joe Lozeau, like most of the other young Indians, was adept at living from the land. This day he suggested we go up to the ditch bank to pick blackcap raspberries. Naturally, Millie and Joe's sister Marian had to tag along. I would have demurred, had not Joe's mother promised me a piece of blackcap raspberry pie. No tame berry makes a pie anywhere near as good as a blackcap raspberry.

If you aren't familiar with blackcap raspberries, there are two facts you should know. Blackcaps are hard to tame, yet will grow readily in the woods wherever man has stirred the earth, in places such as ditch banks and road edges. And blackcap thorns hook downward, and are both long and sharp. Cat claws on a cane.

After half an hour or so of picking, we were doing fine. The girls picked around the edges, while Millie complained of every thorn scratch. Joe and I worked our way into the middle of the patch. Of course, by the time we got through all those canes, we looked like we'd been trying to separate fighting wildcats, but the loss of blood wasn't debilitating.

41

Suddenly, some of the bushes began to shake. We looked up, and something hairy was picking berries on the far side of the patch. Millie, in the manner of timid little girls, assumed the worst.

"B-b-b-bear!"

Disregarding the fact that we were in the middle of a blackcap raspberry patch, we all, of course, panicked— right out through those thorny vines. Joe's dog, a part whippet that could outrun a jackrabbit, was so startled he didn't catch the panic for a few seconds. When he found himself at the rear of the train, he speeded up, even though he had no idea what he was running from. He only held the lead for a short time. I heard something puffing behind me and passed him like a shot.

We ran toward Joe's house shouting, "Bear!" Joe's siblings, seeing our cuts and scratches from the berry vines, assumed the worst and joined in the panic. We ran right through the house and out the back door where Joe's mother was hanging clothes. I had no idea a woman in long full skirts could run so fast. She caught up with Joe and asked what was he running from.

"Bear," he shouted.

"@%$&*#," she said and skidded to a halt. I never could wrap my tongue around the Salish language, but I could recognize cuss words in any tongue. Come to think of it, no bear had ever dared tangle with Mrs. Lozeau.

"Ain't no bear after you."

After we sorted things out, we returned to the berry patch. A nauseating smell assaulted us as we approached.

"Do bears ever smell that bad?" I asked. Joe had more experience with them than I.

"Naw," he said. "That's Old Zeke."

Now I have to tell you about Old Zeke.

Ezekiel Lamb lived alone a mile or so from the Lozeaus. Only the Lozeau family knew much about his past, and the Indians weren't much given to gossip. Encounters by numerous gossipy whites had embellished the stories about Zeke, which were incredible enough on their own.

Dad drove past Zeke's place one below-zero day and noticed there was no smoke from the chimney. Fearing Zeke might be sick or hurt or even dead, Dad stopped to investigate. When his knock and subsequent halloo went unanswered, he searched the house and found no sign of Zeke. He went to the barn and called, and Zeke rose up from his bed in a manger. He had filled the manger with fresh horse manure and put his blankets on it to take advantage of the heat generated as the manure decayed. He stayed warm and cozy there, day and night. Dad said Zeke smelled lots worse than the manure.

Some time later, Zeke did get sick and the Lozeaus took him to the Catholic hospital in Polson. The nuns told Dad about it later. Zeke was so dirty they wanted to give him a bath first thing, but they couldn't get his long johns off. His body hair had grown right through the cloth, and they had to use scissors to cut the hair before they could undress him. Sister Superior, a fine old Irish girl, thought it was probably the highlight of her nursing experience.

Zeke's gone now. I doubt there's a character half as colorful (or smelly) to take his place.

Spuds

I live in Idaho, and I have trouble getting good potatoes unless I go to the small farmers or buy the unusual brands for outrageous prices. What most stores sell as #1 potatoes more often than not have green spots, gouges, bruises or black rot spots. One can rarely find a perfectly good potato.

Fifty or sixty years ago, when Dad raised "spuds" for sale or barter, he didn't rate any potato as #1 if it showed a mark of any kind. He discarded potatoes with green on them whenever he found them. Potato vines are poisonous, and green potatoes are mildly so.

My memories of the acre or so of potatoes that Dad raised are none too pleasant. Planting was odious but perhaps least so of the tasks required to produce potatoes. Not having the specialized mechanical contraptions available nowadays, we did the work by hand. Dad plowed a furrow using a single-bottom horse-drawn walking plow; Mother and I dropped the sections of "seed potato" at intervals; then Dad plowed the seed under. Hard work, but at least we did it standing up.

As the potatoes grew, we plowed between the rows. Lacking more sophisticated equipment, Dad used a single horse and a walking cultivator. I was drafted to lead the old mare as she plodded-plop-plop-along, plowing row after row of potatoes. Sometimes I'd break the monotony and ride, spraddle legged, on her wide back. I suspect my presence was really unnecessary, because the old mare knew how to plow as well as I did. I think Dad just wanted someone to share the monotony and dust.

Again in the fall, Dad turned over the rows of spuds using the same single-bottom plow. Mother and I (and any other luckless individual who could be recruited)

44

followed the plow and picked up the potatoes, putting them into buckets which we carefully emptied into burlap bags. Remember, we didn't want to bruise those spuds or we'd risk Dad's ire, of which he had an inexhaustible supply.

Picking potatoes is one of the less pleasant tasks on the farm. One can't wear gloves (I tried), so the dirt and sweat mix to form a mud. One's fingers become caked with a sandpaper sheen so that rubbing fingers together produces nerve-wracking feelings even worse than those from a fingernail on a blackboard.

The potatoes were carried into the root cellar, one burlap bag at a time. An acre of potatoes produced a lot of bags of potatoes. Until I was in my teens, poor Dad was the only one strong enough to carry those hundred-pound bags down the steps of the cellar. I suppose he made hundreds of trips. I know that, after I became husky enough for the task, I made what seemed like millions .

Dad bartered potatoes wherever he could during the winter. Sometimes he got cattle feed, sometimes human food, and always he paid potatoes for the logs he brought home for firewood. The going cash price, as I remember, was one dollar a hundredweight—a penny a pound. (And to think of the prices I pay now!)

Sometime in late winter, the potatoes got the idea that spring was coming and that it was time to grow. Potato-sprouting time. We handled every remaining potato, brushing the sprouts off and re-sorting the potatoes. The dirt remaining on the potatoes and the juice from the sprouts again formed a coating of gritty mud on our fingers. Talk about putting your teeth on edge!

When I think back, I'm glad to pay the prices I do for potatoes, as long they're washed clean and I don't have to handle that grit.

Crime Of Passion

Stanley was not the type to shoot anyone. He was small for his age, studious and often timid. But when you're fourteen, hate can be a more powerful force than reason.

Stanley hated the school bus. It was the smallest of the set of rickety wooden boxes built on the frames of farm trucks by the farmers who earned a few extra dollars driving the bus routes.

Each year when the school term ended, the boxes were removed from the trucks. They sat among the weeds in barn lots through the summer, havens for mice and sparrows and sometimes an independent brooding hen. The summer odors faded but never completely disappeared, even though joined by the powerful smells of barnyard manure and unwashed children.

In winter, the buses quick-froze their passengers, even packed in as they were; and in the warm days of spring and fall they became ovens in which the children sweat and sweltered and suffered. Why couldn't they have real buses? The school had only one factory-made bus. The school board blamed the depression, but the Crandall school, only ten miles away, had all new "real" buses. It just wasn't fair.

The mud and manure tracked in during the winter dried during the warm spring days; and now, resurrected by the jouncing on the unpaved roads, rose as a cloud of dust, the ghost of past seasons. The dust clogged Stanley's nostrils and forced him to breathe through his mouth. The taste, he thought, was worse than the smell. Well, only another month and school would be out.

Stanley waited while most of the bus passengers crowded into the box. Every day the jibes of the boys on

46

the bus made his ride home more painful. Now they were calling him Stinky Stanley Steinhouse. He wanted to walk home, but whenever he did and came in late, his mother badgered him to find out why.

He wished he could tell his parents about the hell he experienced each day, but the last time he complained, his mother had "got involved" and Stanley had not yet lived that down. His father believed Stanley should take care of these little problems himself. Easy for him to say. His father wasn't a skinny fourteen-year-old. Rather, he was solidly built and could hold his own even with the town bully.

Stanley blinked away tears and, head down, mounted the steps to another doom. Girls and smaller children made way for him as he moved to his rightful place at the back of the bus. He'd rather not have sat there, but custom decreed that the gaggle of eighth grade boys reserve their space on the very back bench.

"Let Stinky in." That from Woody. Woody, the athlete of their class, the strongest, the basketball star. Woody who shot lay-ups easily, while Stanley could barely get the ball to the rim with both hands. Woody, outgoing and bold, was at ease with girls, while Stanley stood completely tongue-tied in their presence. Awed by Stanley's grades, Woody occasionally mentioned them admiringly, proud to have such smart friend. And friend he was—sometimes.

Woody and Stanley lived on adjoining farms. They played and hunted and fished and swam together—unless other boys were about. Then Woody led the teasing. Just today he had snatched Stanley's lunch and started a game of keep-away with it. Stanley had chased the brown bag from one boy to another until, breathless, red-faced and near tears, he had to rest. He had been sitting for only a moment when the bag suddenly appeared in his lap. From the edge of his vision he saw Woody's boots strolling away.

He had barely seated himself on the bench, when one of the group leaned to one side and loudly and deliberately passed gas. A stench filled the air, and the boys' hands fanned their faces.

"Stinky Steinhouse did it again," one of them announced for the whole bus to hear.

"I *didn't*," Stanley howled.

"Who else?"

"Stinky did it," announced the real perpetrator with a smirk.

"Stinky, you hadn't ought to do that," said Woody, laughing. "Why, those poor girls up there—look at them. They can hardly keep from puking." Indeed, several of the girls were looking at Stanley with disdain. "What did you have in your lunch, Stinky? A bean sandwich?"

Stanley charged his tormentor, but the other boys pulled him off and held him. Fighting on the bus was subject to immediate and irrefutable punishment of all involved, and several of the boys had many miles to walk.

The bus stopped at Stanley's farm, and the boys let him go. He tripped as he walked to the front of the bus—and from Woody's smirk, he knew it was not the accident it appeared to be.

As the bus pulled away, Woody opened a window and called to him.

"Good night, Stinky. Maybe you better check your pants to see if that one was dry." The window slammed shut and Stanley heard howls of laughter as the bus pulled away. He stood at the edge of the road, quaking from his fury at the final taunt. The rage, the hot pain and frustration slowly metamorphosed into cold, calculating hatred. He'd fix Woody. He'd fix them all. They'd see. All he had to do was kill Woody and the teasing would stop.

His decision made, he immediately became purposeful. He needed a weapon. His memory pictured a long slim knife, a stiletto buried in an old trunk his father kept in the barn. He had only seen into the trunk once, accidentally, and had earned a lecture.

"That's a badman's knife," his father had said. "It's the kind some slick hombre keeps up his sleeve. That kind of knife is too easy to use. Like a pistol. If a guy gets mad, it's too easy to use a pistol—and even if you're right, you might do something you'll regret forever. I won't own a pistol. Not since—let's get out of here." He closed the trunk and stood bent as if under a great burden, looking incredibly sad.

After supper that night Stanley, still curious, had asked his father, "How'd you come by the stiletto?"

"Manfred!" His mother seldom spoke that sharply to his father. Stanley looked up at her. She was pale as skim milk, her lips clamped in a rigid line.

"Never ask that again," his father said. His tone was such that Stanley never had. For weeks he dreamed scenario after scenario, in each trying to imagine his father the hero. It never seemed to work. After a time he dropped the knife from his mind. Until today.

Now, the stiletto seemed like a solution. He'd get the knife. His father had said it could be hidden up a sleeve. Once he'd taken care of Woody, the rest would leave him alone. He'd be dangerous. He'd be a *badman.*

He walked directly to the barn. The familiar smells of harness leather and hay and manure both old and fresh, made the place seem comfortingly familiar. Today he didn't want their comfort. Today he wanted to nurse the bitterness within him, and to savor his dream of revenge.

49

He left the door to the dark storage room open; still, in the dim light, he had to bend over and peer closely to identify the contents of the trunk. He held the stiletto up in the meager light and a stone fell in his stomach. The knife was rusted and dull, and useless for what he planned unless he spent hours cleaning and sharpening the blade. He did not have hours. He must act now or lose his resolve.

A shadow darkened the room, and he dropped the knife and closed the trunk lid guiltily. His father stood in the doorway. "Looking for something?"

"No. No. Just fooling around."

"Don't go fooling around in that trunk. I told you before. Come on out of there. Now."

Stanley followed his father out silently, his mind racing for some other way to exact the revenge his bitterness demanded.

He couldn't find a pistol, but he could still use a gun. He had his own .22 caliber rifle—it was in the kitchen. He felt sure he could sneak it out. A large irrigation canal led from his father's fields right to Woody's house. He could sneak up the ditch without anyone seeing him.

Stanley opened the battered screen door quietly and tiptoed into the house, knowing that he had to avoid his mother's inquisitive looks. He slid the .22 out of its rack and picked up a box of cartridges. Long rifles. They penetrated much better. He closed the screen door carefully, and ran quickly behind the barn. From there he could walk unobserved to the big canal.

Sloshing and slipping along the muddy canal bed, Stanley rejoiced that it was too early in the spring for irrigation. He had only an occasional puddle to wade. He crept along bent almost double, making sure he could not be seen. It seemed to take him forever to slog along so that he came opposite Woody's house.

Stanley peeked through last year's weeds and found he was in luck. Woody worked in the garden only a few yards from the ditch. Stanley lay half-in, half-out of the ditch until he caught his breath. He brought the rifle up and aimed at where he thought Woody's heart should be. Maybe the .22 wasn't powerful enough to penetrate. Maybe he should shoot at Woody's neck or his eye. He thought of the times he and Woody had discussed how to shoot at a vulnerable spot, how to squeeze, not pull.

A sharp whistle sounded in front of him and to his left. A gopher! The first ground squirrel of the year. Stanley thought it was early for them to be out. He turned slowly to scan the bank and finally saw the squirrel's head just poking above the ground. Its profile was so close Stanley count the lashes around its eye. So many times he and Woody had hunted the ubiquitous gophers together. Woody was his best friend—and his worst enemy. Stanley swallowed a sob as the tears flooded his eyes. He laid his head down to clear his eyes and recover his resolve. He had to shoot.

Stanley aimed as carefully as ever he had. At this distance, an eye was such an easy target. He squeezed carefully. The .22 cracked. He dropped the gun and fled along the ditch, tear-blinded, sobbing uncontrollably. When he reached the spot where he had entered the ditch, he climbed out and lay on the grass and retched.

When he finally sat up and wiped his mouth and eyes, he calmed himself by thinking: What I've done, I've done.

Feeling unbelievably tired, he trudged back to the house. Supper was ready, and much as he felt like skipping it, he managed to eat a few bites lest his mother question him. The meal over, his father leaned back in his

51

chair and began to pick his teeth. He stopped, frowned, and said, "Stan, where's the .22?"

Stanley felt his face go white. The gun. He dropped it when he shot. Now his father would know. God, how dumb could he be? How could he explain, where was his excuse? Tongue-tied in his terror, Stanley hardly noticed a car drive up to the house. A knock on the door interrupted his frantic mental search for an alibi.

"Well, hi, Jim," his father boomed.

"Hello, Manny." It was Jim Woodson. Woody's father. "Manny, is this Stan's gun?" he asked softly.

"Yeah. Sure is. Where'd you get it?"

"Found it on the ditch bank at my place."

Woody crowded in past his father. "Hey, Stan. I saw the gopher you shot. Nice shot. Right in the eye. But why'd you leave the gun there?"

Stanley could only shake his head.

"Hey, Stan, listen. Boy, will we give ole Bill Caulkins a razzing on the bus Monday. He was—wait." His voice dropped to a whisper. "Let's go outside." He nodded sideways to indicate their parents, then led the way to the door.

Entrepreneur

I was fourteen the first time I went into business. I didn't make much money, but I generated enough good will to stand me in good stead during my later, wilder teens. It may have even kept me out of the arms of the local law.

You may remember, if you read my article called "Poor Visibility,"[3] that, when fog blacked out our farm in the winter of 1939-40, I climbed to the roof of the house to see why we had no daylight. When I reached the gable and stood up, I stuck my head through several inches of snow. The fog was so thick the snow couldn't fall through it.

Now for the rest of the story.

I climbed down and told Dad what was going on. Although I have always told the absolute truth, in this case he just didn't believe me. He still had a hard time believing me after he climbed up to see for himself.

Back on the ground, I hunted up my skis and a shovel and took them back up onto the snow. With skis on, I was able to move around on the snow, and shovel paths to the outbuildings in the order of their importance—the outhouse, the barn and the chicken house. I got careless after a while, and let one ski slide off the snow onto the cleared path. The fog alone wouldn't support the ski, and I almost fell through. From then on, I was very careful to keep my skis on solid snow.

Those paths in the snow let in enough light for us to feel our way around the barn lot. On the ground, we had to take care not to get away from the light track, because if

---

[3] See "Poor Visibility," *Building Character: Tales from Montana (And Other Damn Lies)* page 118.

we got out into the complete blackness we'd not know where the heck we were.

Dad and I talked the situation over after we finished the chores. If I could shovel paths for us, I could do so for neighbors. I argued that if I had a tractor that could travel over the snow, I could really clear a barn lot and could charge for it. Dad was reluctant to agree to charging for a neighborly act, but he agreed that if someone ran a tractor, he ought to be paid something.

Remember, the valley sloped north to south. I put on my skis and skied north until I reached the edge of the fog. Wes Halverson had a Caterpillar with a bulldozer blade, but I passed him up. I thought the 'dozer might get him too close to the edge of the snow and I didn't want to be responsible for the outfit falling on someone.

I knew Arnie Dickson, a mile or so away from the edge of the fog, had a Cat with a skip loader so I skied over and asked Arnie if we could form a partnership. Arnie was skeptical. He could see the snow and could tell the fog was really thick; but even though he admitted I had skied to his place, he wondered if the snow would hold his Cat. Finally, I talked him into trying the tractor on the snow.

He moved cautiously out onto the fog. He found the Cat could indeed travel all right on the snow, although the fog underneath sagged a little, making it seem like he was driving across a water bed. Of course, Arnie didn't realize that—water beds as we know them hadn't been invented yet. If someone had mentioned "water bed" to him, he'd have thought of a leaky tent in elk season. Arnie agreed to give our partnership a try. I remembered to warn him to keep off the cleared areas. I didn't want that tractor crashing through onto one of our clients.

Not surprisingly, when we drove to a farm and offered to clear paths so the farmer could do his chores, we were more than welcome. Most farmers forced money on us, and we made eight dollars and thirty-one cents each (quite a bit of money in those days) clearing the snow above the farmers' barn lots and feedlots.

The trouble with those paths didn't show up for a while. A day or so after I made them, the sun got warm enough to start melting the snow on top. The melt water ran down onto the fog which sagged to form little pockets. The water in some of those pockets formed lenses, and the sun shining through a lens suddenly melted some of the fog. If you were walking along a light track underneath when that happened, sploosh—ice water down the back of your neck. Very disconcerting when you're stumbling along in almost total darkness.

Eventually, the snow melted, and most of the fog thinned out, although some hung out in a few low places down by the coulee well into spring. When the county road crews started fixing the roads, they were short of money, so they sawed the last of the remaining fog into slabs and used it for forms when they were pouring concrete culverts. They didn't have to come out and take up these forms. The hot summer sun eventually dissipated the fog and the forms simply melted away.

Fog worked well for forms, although it had a tendency to bulge a little in a few places. I can still show you those bulges in the concrete culverts to this day.

Chinook

Last night the snow crunched beneath our feet, and the stars hung just above the ground. Eyelashes froze in tears, and noses ran. We banked the old wood stove and burrowed under stacks of quilts against the cold. Sometime in the night we woke too warm, and wondering why, we threw off the covers. This morning, the sound of water dripping from the eaves and the whistle of the south wind that blew warm rain all night tell us that the January thaw has come. The snow, sixteen inches deep yesterday, is giving ground to the warm breath of the Princess Chinook.

The trees have shed their white robes; they flex their branches in the wind as if relieved to be freed of the burdens of snow and cold. They stand outlined dark green against a hillside backdrop, mottled by splotches of bare ground among the drifts. In stubble fields last year's straw pokes bravely through the snow, and fields plowed late in the fall are zebra-striped in black loam and snowy furrow. The wind ripples the surface of the meltwater puddles on our walkway, and where the water overflows, the rills tinkle down the walks and tunnel under the snow. Birds rejoice at their feeders, calling to one another and flitting about no longer concerned with anything but the serious business of feeding.

Winter may not be over, but the promise of spring is here.

The Jackalope

Some city dude who writes for the Spokane newspaper—in order to educate the tourist trade, he said—stated categorically that "jackalopes do not exist." I take exception. Just because he has never seen a jackalope in the wild he still has no justification for such pedantry. And such proclamations from the ignorant have an extremely detrimental effect on tourists' perception of our veracity. I wish to make it plain that jackalopes *do* exist and can still be found in several western states.

For those who have never traveled the West, a jackalope looks a great deal like a jackrabbit, except the jackalope sports antlers. There are two subspecies. The extremely rare subspecies which gave the beast its name has horns very much like those of the pronghorn antelope of the West. I have not seen—nor even heard of—any of this family for thirty-odd years, and they may indeed be extinct.

The other, more common, variety may indeed be extinct in the more civilized states of Washington and Oregon; but, though they are rare, they can still be found in parts of Montana, Idaho, Wyoming and Texas. This subspecies has larger horns, somewhat like the antlers of a mule deer.

A jackalope can outrun a jackrabbit any day. I once scared up both at the same time, and the jackalope was long gone before I could take a shot. Of course, a jackrabbit takes a high jump every few hops, which may slow him down, but makes him a very hard target. I used to hit only seven out of ten jack-rabbits with my .22.

When I was a youth, jackalopes were plentiful in many parts of Montana, Idaho, Oregon and even in central Washington around Moses Lake. Because of human encroachment on their semi-desert habitat—irrigation and housing developments are the worst culprits—much of their normal range has been destroyed and the survivors have moved on to browner, as it were, pastures. In the still-dry areas though, magpies are a problem. Once he gets a taste of jackalope eggs, a magpie will leave a three-day-dead skunk to rob a jackalope nest.

Back in the not-so-Great Depression, when we had little to eat (even though we lived on a farm) we ate whatever meat came our way—blackbirds, groundhog and porcupine, among other things. Porcupine is a delicacy I hope you have had the good fortune to miss, as I have stated before.[4] Jackalope meat, on the other hand, is tasty. Like chicken.

It was about 1932, as I remember, Dad stumbled upon a jackalope nest. Believing that any old meat is better than none, he took the young 'lopes home, intending to try breeding and raising them. He was at least partially successful. The jackalopes thrived, although feeding them was a chore, since in the wild their principal food is a type of scrub similar to sage brush only smaller and tougher. We called it "rabbit brush". Rabbit brush grows on semi-arid wasteland throughout the West, including the unirrigated land in the Flathead Valley, and Dad harvested whatever and wherever he could.

He kept the jackalopes in a chicken-wire enclosure which completely surrounded them. Even the floor and the top of the pen were chicken wire. The floor kept the 'lopes from digging their way out, and the wire over the top of the pen kept them from jumping to freedom. There the jackalopes' antlers presented a problem. The female jackalope's horns are usually only spikes, but the male grows branching antlers. When the horns of the male jackalope begin to grow, they are actually much like the pronghorn antelope horns of the rarer cousins, but as they mature, most grow out to be deerlike. A jackalope that survives coyotes, hunters, Montana winters and greyhound buses for a few years may have horns with five or six points. A word of caution—if you see jackalope road

---

[4]See "On Eating Porcupine," *Building Character:Tales from Montana (And Other Damn Lies)* page 17.

kill, avoid it. Those horns can puncture a steel-belted radial.

Dad began his jackalope experiment using inch-and-a-half-mesh chicken wire over the pen. However, when the jackalopes jumped against the covering they were forever catching their horns in the chicken wire. A jackalope's hind legs are terrifically strong, and are a potent weapon. Many a hunting dog has been ruined when he/she was sent to track a jackalope. The 'lope will outrun the dog easily, then double back and cross the dog's path. He will jump over the dog and deliver a kick fierce enough to down Joe Louis. When his head stops spinning and his eyes uncross and his ears stop ringing, a dog with any sense says, "To hell with it," and is content to lie by the fire and leave the hunting to others.

Keep in mind those terrible hind legs when you imagine two jackalopes hanging by their horns and struggling to get free. Such a pair would damage each other so badly that whatever meat was left was hardly fit for consumption. Dad was forced to use finer and finer mesh wire, until he found a mesh too small to entangle jackalope horns. What finally worked was screen liberated from an abandoned gold sluice. The price was right, too.

Dad kept jackalopes for food for a number of years. Our Sunday dinners were often stewed jackalope with beans, although the jackalope was usually just a little bit tough and Mother had to start cooking the jackalope on Friday night in order to get it done for Sunday dinner.

By the time I went away to war in 1943, Dad had switched from jackalopes to Mother's chickens for our Sunday dinners on the hoof. Besides being much tenderer meat, chickens are a lot easier to corral when they escape from a pen, and Dad could raise or buy feed for them rather than having to harvest rabbit brush. Also, the magpie population exploded about that time and gathering enough wild jackalope eggs for a setting before the magpies got them was too much trouble and took too much of Dad's time away from fishing and tall-tale-telling with his cronies. For a few years, he kept a a couple of jackalopes for old times' sake, but he gave them up before I came back after the war.

Although some of my rancher friends in Montana still speak fondly and proudly of the jackalopes on their range, I myself have not seen a jackalope for years. Mostly, I think, because I have been stuck in cities away from the less-inhabited areas of the West. The last live jackalope I saw was one my headlights caught sitting beside the road south of my home town of Charlo one Sunday morning at a few minutes after one o'clock in the morning. I am sure of the time because I had just left the bar in Charlo when it closed, as always, at one o'clock, after a big and rowdy Saturday night.

Recently, Chanci Fulwiler of Haugen, Montana, told me that attempts at crossing jackalopes with ring-necked pheasants have been at least partially successful. Chanci goes to college in Jamestown, North Dakota, and I suppose that's where the breeding program is situated. I saw a specimen of the flying jackalope, and it seemed to me that the poor thing flies about as well as one of our old hens, being able to get off the ground only a few feet and able to fly only fifty yards or so. Perhaps further experiments will result in a truly challenging game animal that can fly with the speed of a pheasant and run like an earth-bound jackalope.

61

They Call It a Game

In my adult years, I have several times been invited to learn the game of golf. For many years I pooh-poohed the idea, saying I'd take up golf when I was too old to chase anything but a little white ball. Now that I've reached that age (well, almost), it's time for me to confess the real reason I avoid the game. One of the hard lessons I learned, meandering dazedly through puberty, is this: golf is a dangerous and sometimes deadly game. The very thought of playing gives me a headache, and a recurring pain in my ribs.

When I was in my early teens, a girl named Lorelei lived on the farm near ours. The original Lorelei, you may remember, was a siren. This Lorelei definitely was not. It's hard to describe her, but when I recall her figure, Rosie Grier comes to mind. And her face—well, maybe like Hulk Hogan's, but with more facial hair. It was a face that not even a mother could love, which might have been the reason Lorelei spent a lot of time at our house.

One day, Lorelei informed me that I was her boyfriend. That was a fate I had to deny. When I got up from the ground, I wiped my bloody nose and said, "OK."

Lorelei got her hands on a book about golf, and read and re-read it until she became obsessed with the game, and though she didn't admit it, the figures of the lovely and lissome ladies who played it. Nothing would do but she learn the game, no doubt hoping that she would develop a lovely and lissome figure, too. Fat chance. Since I was her boyfriend, I must play golf too. Or else. Never mind that there wasn't a course within thirty miles, and even if there had been, we couldn't have, between us, scraped up enough for a caddie tip, let alone green fees. Never mind that we couldn't afford even one much-used golf club, let alone a set apiece. We were going to play golf. Lorelei gathered up an old branding iron for a driver, tied an old tablespoon to a broomstick, hunted up a shillelagh-like cedar branch, and trimmed an old hockey stick down a bit. She had golf clubs. What the heck. In the '30's, we "made do" so often I rather admired her ingenuity. That was all I admired about her.

Lorelei had to be content with a course of her own making. She laid out nine holes that had more hazards than all the present golf courses in the state of Montana, and maybe Idaho, as well. She chose the "greens" where the cows had cropped the grass short. There were water hazards aplenty—all the irrigation ditches and a fast-running stream in the coulee near the third hole. There weren't any sand traps, but fresh cowpies were plentiful on the "fairways." She declared the course a par 41. I didn't have any idea what that meant, but I found I could play three holes or so in forty-one strokes, and I participated for that long, then looked for an excuse to quit.

Lorelei was a demon for the "play it where it lies" rule. No dropping a ball for a one-stroke penalty with her. Whenever I had to drive out of a cowpie trap, I wished fervently the farm had been built on sand. Sometimes, when I felt like living dangerously, I used her "spoon" to exit the trap and made sure she enjoyed the "divot", too. I had to run like hell when I did that.

The most serious danger of playing golf was revealed one hot July day when Lorelei was having a bad round. I'd had a good second hole, with only ten strokes, and she was only six strokes up on me. I teed off for the third hole, and shanked the ball into the cattails down by the coulee. That was sure to be a bad lie because that was where the cows tried to stay cool on such a day. I was strolling around trying to think up a good way of getting out of playing the rest of the day, when I kicked up a hen pheasant just as Lorelei swung. Her ball went about where mine had, and the driver (branding iron) came whistling by my head.

"Find the balls," she said.

"Yes, Master." I ran toward the cattail patch.

I found only one ball, hers. It had bounced up and was stuck just under the base of a cow's tail. The cow, a gentle Jersey milch cow, didn't seem to mind at all. Giggling to myself, I thought, I'll make her play this one where it lies.

When Lorelei arrived, red-faced, and puffing, I lifted the cow's tail triumphantly and said, "This looks like yours."

I was looking at her expression and didn't notice that the ball had already dropped to the ground. I hope you have heard Bill Cosby's accurate description of a conniption. Lorelei's conniption was the last thing I remember.

By the time my ribs had healed and I had stopped seeing double, Lorelei had given up golf, and had found a new boyfriend, poor devil. To tell the truth, all that pain was worth it. I was OUT.

Yes, golf is a dangerous game. Way, way too dangerous for me.

Fish Story

Some of my readers (you know who you are) have asked why I haven't included some fish stories in my books. I have my reasons. You think all fish stories are lies, and I don't want to tarnish my credibility. I have relented in this book, and the fish stories I have to tell are the absolute truth, although this story is so extraordinary that even I sometimes have trouble believing it. However, now that I've firmly established my reputation for veracity, I think you will understand.

I guess I arrived in the West after all the big fish had been caught. The tales I heard indicated that was the case. So, according to the local old-timers, the biggest fish I ever caught—or, rather, helped catch—was just a minnow.

I understand sturgeon are now classified as an endangered species in the rivers of Montana; but when I was younger, they were plentiful and the Flathead River was a fine fishing ground. The sturgeon in the river were

65

phenomenal. Dad and I used a trot-line tied to trees on both sides of the river which, at that point, was only a couple hundred yards wide at high-water marks. The line hung three baits.

Most of the time, when we hooked a sturgeon, we could get several strong guys to help and pull it ashore. Not much finesse—just drag her up onto the sand. Some of the sturgeon were so big that three men couldn't handle them. We could always tell if we got a big one on the line by how tight the rope across the river was. We kept a saddled horse around, and when the tree holding the trot-line was shaking like a high wind, we'd throw a dally round the saddle horn and pull the fish out with the saddle horse.

We pulled out our biggest fish ever while Granddad was visiting. Granddad was always a great fisherman, having lived along the Skunk River in Iowa. He told tales of the big catfish in the river and of fishing for them with a pick handle. When the Skunk overflowed, he claimed walked high and dry along the raised railroad tracks, and when he saw a rustling among the cornstalks, he slipped out and clobbered the big old channel catfish with the pick handle. Channel cat are great eating.

When our big sturgeon finally came up into the shallows, thrashing and flopping and then skidded up the rocky beach, Granddad was impressed. Without water, the fish couldn't get purchase, so it was nearly helpless. A half dozen dogs stood around watching the excitement, and one old dog thought he could show his mettle, now that the fish was powerless. The sturgeon's flapping tail threw him halfway across the river. Must have made him deaf, too—no matter how much we called him he wouldn't come back to our side of the river.

That fish almost did Granddad in—not from any direct action, but Granddad got so excited we thought he'd burst a blood vessel. We hauled that fish up into our old farm wagon. With the nose against the front, the tail hung out and slapped every rock of any size the wagon straddled. Granddad looked like he'd bust his buttons, sitting up there when he drove that wagon into town.

My fishing buddies quit me when we tied into the really big fish. We knew he was a whopper—the trot-line was shaking the trees like a hurricane. We tied on the saddle horse, and tried to drag the fish out. The fish, for his part, tried to drag the pony in, and was doing a good job of it, too. The horse leaned against that rope until he was almost on his belly, but he couldn't hold his footing, and started sliding backward into the river. That fish was on his way to drowning the horse and the cowboy, too, but the horse stumbled and rolled so the cowhand could cut loose. The rope across the river held, so we were able to get a log chain on the line. We unhitched the team from the wagon and hooked them to the chain. They dug in, and slowly pulled the sturgeon toward shore. It wasn't easy. That log chain was so tight you could hit high E if you touched it. Then the line broke and the team fell on their noses. Luckily, the end of the rope was out in the water, so it was damped or it would have cut one or two of us in half. Even hampered by the water, the end whipped around and splintered a good-sized rock, spraying us with shards of granite. When the excitement settled down, my friends decided that kind of fishing was getting too goldarn dangerous, and quit on me. Alone, I had to give up, but that one that got away sure must have been a monster.

The Toboggan

It was the Fourth of July. Rather than spend the day making hay as we usually did on July 4th, Dad opted for a picnic at MacDonald Lake in the Mission Mountains. My last minute effort to find a suitable companion for the day failed miserably, so I settled on Elroy Blurch. Elroy was a walking disaster waiting to happen. He didn't disappoint me this day.

After a great picnic dinner, Elroy and I set out exploring. MacDonald Lake is dammed—the water is used for irrigation. We walked up the dam to the spillway and, wondering about the swimming possibilities, I reached down to try the water with a toe. I have never seen nor felt such cold water since. I recoiled a step backward. Unfortunately, one step backward brought me to a large stinging nettle plant.

When my body sensed the nettles, it reacted again, this time propelling me forward *two* steps—into the icy water. I don't think I yelled. Unconcerned with commenting, I concentrated on getting out of that water, but by the time I turned and swam back to the concrete edge, I had lost control of my voluntary muscles. My body was on automatic pilot and I dog-paddled against the concrete wall, unable to command my arms to pull me out. Elroy reached down and dragged me onto the bank.

"What'd you do that for?" he asked.

"N-n-n-nettles," I said.

He looked at the nettle bush.

"Oh." And that was the end of our swimming.

The temperature was well over ninety that day. but my body didn't care. It was cold all day.

Since we declined to go swimming, we sought other entertainment. A good trail ran along one side of the lake, but the sketchy deer trail on the other side looked to us to be more entertaining. We slipped and slid along the deer trail until we reached a long bank of shale lying over the trail. When we stepped on the shale, we found it very unstable—the rocks began to slide down toward the lake. Each time we started a rock, several feet of shale surface slid a few feet.

Climbing above the shale was hot work, but I still wasn't warm and couldn't sweat. Makes for hard climbing. When we reached the top of the slide, a shale cliff rose above us. If we wished to continue around the lake, we'd have to cross the slide. We started out gingerly, keeping close to the cliff face, and only infrequently stepping on the slide. Each time we did touch the slide, several tons of rock moved downhill. Halfway across, the shale lay close up against the cliff.

Elroy went first, tiptoeing from rock to rock and holding onto the cliff face. When he was most of the way across, he called to me to come on, so I started across, copying his steps as best I could.

Somewhere near halfway, I lost my balance and placed my whole weight on a single large sheet of rock. The rock started moving, the shale underneath moved too, and soon I was tobogganing down the slide. I knew I couldn't stay upright, so I dropped to my hands and knees and held on for dear life. The moving rocks around me generated a cloud of dust so I could hardly see. Had I been able to understand my predicament, I might have been scared. As it was, I was only moderately terrified.

After a century or two, the moving rocks came to a halt and catapulted me forward—into the icy lake. This time, I was able to control my arms enough to swim to the edge of the slide, just in time to hear a whoop and see a new slide, with Elroy riding a large slab *standing up*. He whooped all the way down, until his carriage slid right into the water. When he hit the cold water, his whoop was cut off as if with scissors, and he came swimming furiously to where I waited. I helped him from of the water as he had helped me. He stood there shivering and trying to shake circulation back into his hands.

"Have fun?" I asked.

"@#%@$%," he said.

To tell the truth, he wasn't nearly so much fun as we scrambled our way to the end of the lake and returned by the better trail.

Family Feud

In one large family I knew, the boys and the girls feuded continually. Sound familiar? This family lived in an old two-story farmhouse, without electricity or indoor plumbing. One day the boys sneaked upstairs and put effervescent salts in the empty chamber pots. The girls who used them that night got quite a surprise. Knowing the boys didn't use chamber pots but got up and went outside, the girls retaliated by putting flypaper at the foot of the stair the next night. The boys asked for a truce.

Time For A Change

I'm not sure when I actually became a dirty old man, but I know for sure it was before I was eighteen. Maria may not have been a major influence, but she gave me one of the first shoves toward that destiny. Not that she had to shove very hard.

I met Maria when I was not quite sixteen. Her father owned a traveling threshing rig, and I worked with his crew for a few days. Easygoing enough ordinarily, the old man was a hellion when it came to protecting Maria. None of the men on the crew dared make any sort of pass at her, and she seemed not to notice them. To me, an old lady of twenty-three was an enigma. She never cursed like the men, but she didn't turn a hair when the filthiest word reached her ears. She couldn't have weighed a hundred twenty pounds, but when it came to pitching bundles, she stacked up to any of the men. We talked a little as we worked, but our conversations were mostly just a "Hi!" and a smile. At dinner (noon, on the farm) she managed to sit by me and once or twice she complimented me on being able to hold my own on the crew. But she never talked about Maria.

Came Saturday night and, as usual, there was a dance in town. Most of the crew were old worn-out married men, and a dance interested them not a bit. Some might go to a nearby bar to hoist a few beers and shoot pool, but they never partied enough to interfere with the next day's work. Besides, their wives hadn't let them bring along any duds fancy enough for a dance.

Maria wanted to go to the dance, and knowing the men were afraid of her father, she asked me to take her. I really didn't want to go like a date, she being so old. I knew there would be gossip and I'd take a ton of ribbing from my friends. But Maria had treated me okay and I

71

felt like she was sort of a sister (well, maybe a cousin) and I ought to be nice to her. Besides, my father raised me to do whatever was necessary to make a lady happy, so I agreed to go.

We cleaned up the best we could (washed our hands and faces, that is) and started the long walk across the fields to town. The sliver of new moon lighted the way for us so we could at least keep from falling in the ditches and running into fences.

Maria didn't talk, so I kept my mouth shut except to warn her of hazards such as cowpies.

At the edge of town, we cut through the Goldmans' yard. I knew the Goldmans weren't home. They were our local token Jewish family, who drove to Missoula Friday and stayed until Sunday morning, a situation I deplored since it drastically reduced the availability of the beautiful Naomi Goldman for social life.

The Goldmans' collie came out to greet us. Of course, I knew every dog in town and every dog knew me, so I called Chester by name and he came over for the ear-scratching I always gave. Evidently, Mrs. Goldman was off-beat about her weekly schedule, too, and didn't follow the commonly accepted routine that required Monday be wash day. Her clothesline sagged with newly washed clothing, most of it already dry. Maria looked at a pretty dress, and wished aloud she had something to wear besides her dusty overalls. I was shocked when she took the dress from the line, but I didn't say anything. After all, Maria was much, much older than I. She held the dress against her, and it looked like a good fit. When I thought about it, Naomi Goldman was about Maria's size.

"I'm gonna borrow this," she said.

I gulped, and tried to speak, but my heart wasn't in it. Instead, it was making quick trips from the pit of my stomach to my throat.

"Grab some pants and a shirt," Maria whispered.

Jerry Goldman was about my size, and the temptation was too great. I took down his best pants.

"What now?" I asked.

"We better clean up some more," Maria said. "Let's go back to that ditch and wash and change. Wish we had some soap."

Again, even before I became a dirty old man, I was a gentleman. If a lady expressed a wish, it was my duty to fulfill it. I had been to Goldmans' a number of times, and I knew that they kept a wash basin and soap on the porch. Most folks then had no running water, and the back porch served the same purpose as the bathroom sink does for most people today. Chester made no objection when I went onto the porch and filched the soap and the not-so-clean hand towel. After all, I'd already committed one crime, so one or two more wouldn't make much difference.

At the ditch, Maria started taking off her shirt.

"You go over there," she pointed. "And don't look."

Up to that point, I hadn't really thought of Maria as a *girl* girl, and, until right then the idea of looking at her taking a bath hadn't entered my head. But with that thought came another. *She* might look at *me!*

I scrambled along the bank until she was an indistinct blot in the dark. I hoped she couldn't see me.

After a quick bath, I donned Jeremy's clothes and crept back to Maria. Naomi's dress fit her. Perhaps it fit her too well. I realized for the first time that Maria had a figure to be reckoned with, and the dress, which I guess was called a dirndl, showed a magnificent cleavage, outstanding even in the weak moonlight.

"Did you peek?" Maria asked.

"Uh. No. Of course not."

Maria reached over and pinched my cheek.

"Su-u-u-re," she said.

We left our work clothes on the bank and followed the sounds of the band to the school gymnasium. At the door, Maria stopped me.

"Wait a minute," she said, "introduce me to a woman—that one."

I did. Carol Jensen was about her age, and Maria whispered to her. Carol looked her over quickly, and her eyes stopped at that cleavage. Her lips pursed disapprovingly.

"Oh," she said, "we don't have such a thing. But there's a mirror in the boys' locker room. We call *that* the powder room."

When Maria disappeared in the direction she pointed, I struck up an aimless conversation with Scott Free, one of the local cowboys. Maria and was soon back. From somewhere she'd gotten lipstick, and she'd combed her hair. Scott whistled softly. I guess she did look pretty good. She started to lead me inside, but Scott stopped us.

"Hey, Dick, old pal. Introduce me to the lady?"

"Uh, Maria, this is Scott Free," I said, "Scott, this is Maria, uh, gosh, uh—." I knew her name was Smith or Jones or Brown or something like that but I couldn't ever remember which.

"Lipkowitz," Maria offered. I must have looked startled because Maria elbowed me in the ribs.

"Can I have this dance, Miss Lipswitch?" Scott wasn't exactly one of those shy cowboys.

Maria grabbed his arm. "Call me Maria," she said, and they danced away.

I spent most of the next couple of hours in the stag line, although once or twice I got up enough nerve to ask a girl to dance. Every time I saw Maria on the floor she was dancing with a different partner, most often with one of the young married farmers. There seemed to be a lot of young wives pouting in the wallflower corner, but I didn't realize what their problem was until after I'd been married a while myself.

I was having a smoke outside when Maria came out, propelled by one of the local Lotharios. He'd had enough to drink to make him think he was another Clark Gable or whoever, and seemed to be manhandling her along.

"C'mon to the car and have a drink," he said.

Maria stopped, but he tried to drag her along. I knew what the gentleman's code required, so I stepped forward to rescue her, prepared to die a hero's death. This guy weighed twice what I did and would kill me with his first punch. Before I could start my suicide run, there was a whirlwind of activity, and Maria marched back into the gym, leaving her erstwhile swain retching in a fetal position, blood pouring from his nose. I sighed with relief. Maria certainly didn't need any knight in shining armor.

I danced with Maria twice. The first time, she grabbed me for the supper dance. "Supper" was cookies and punch, and a time for socializing. Someone bumped my arm and I spilled my punch, spotting Naomi's dress and Jerry's pants. Maria wiped it off quickly, and never seemed to see it again.

When the band played "The Waltz You Saved for Me," indicating that the evening was over, Maria came over and took my arm again. Before I knew it, I was dancing better than I ever had, although my thoughts (and my eyes) were occupied with the canyon of the frontage before me.

"Don't stare," Maria whispered. "I've had enough of that from every other man here tonight." Every other *man*. Wow!

As the dance broke up and the crowd began drifting away, Maria and I started home. The Goldmans still weren't home, so we undressed by the clothesline and hung up our appropriated apparel. I tried a peek.

"Don't look!" Maria said sharply. She needn't have. In the weak starlight I couldn't see *anything* but a dim outline. Darn. We felt around at the ditch bank until we found our own clothing.

We made our way "home" mostly by stumble and feel. We had no catastrophes, although twice we came up against barb wire fences without warning. This time, Maria talked. She told me she had a husband and baby at her mama's house in Texas, but she'd traveled from Texas to Canada working on her daddy's threshing rig every harvest season since she was fourteen. She could make more money in a season than she could a whole year at a regular job. Tonight she'd been lonesome for her baby, and getting away for the dance had helped. She thanked me, said she'd asked me to go with her because I reminded her of her brother who'd been my age when he died.

I had to ask.

"Why did you tell Scott your name was Lipkowitz? I thought it was Jones, or something. "

"That's my dad's name, and my maiden name. If I told him my married name—Gonzales—how would the locals have treated me? In Texas, half the folks I know have Spanish names, but up here—"

I saw what she meant. Spanish names in our area meant manual labor imported from Mexico or the Philippines, and some of the locals were pretty snooty about them, although all through school Joe Rosario and Juan Padilla were two of my best friends.

When we came to the farm buildings where the threshing crew slept, Maria issued a final warning.

"Don't you ever, ever tell anybody about any of tonight," she whispered. I remembered the Romeo lying on the ground in his own blood and puke and promised most sincerely. Maria kissed my cheek and climbed onto the bed of her daddy's truck where she slept, and I went off to make a bed in the straw under a wagon.

Sunday night, the threshing crew moved on without me, and I never saw Maria again.

On Monday I heard Mrs. Goldman berating the storekeeper about the laundry soap he sold. She was not happy.

"I washed Naomi's best dress and Jeremy's summer pants, and they looked fine, but when they dried they had stains on them, like they'd had juice spilled. What kind of stain would just disappear when I washed it, then come back when they dried? What kind of soap do you have that will take it out?"

I wondered, "What would Maria say?"

Permanent Sit-uation?

Cornelius Frump
Has grown to a stump.
He's sat there for many a year.
His color is good—
That's, if you like wood—
And if sitting's a decent career.

77

Range Fire

The notion that sheep eat grass down to the roots and therefore kill pasturage was the basis for many of the cattlemen-sheepmen wars of the Old West. When I was a youth, most of the old-time cowmen I knew considered sheep the ruination of the range. Few of them admitted that when it comes to devastating range, a sheep doesn't hold a candle to a hungry horse. Sheep eat grass down to the roots. A horse will eat everything above ground and then paw up the roots and eat them too. And sometimes go beyond that.

I guess Dad thought I needed experience. He sent me east of the mountains to the Choteau country to help out on the ranch owned by his old-time friend Jesse Harding. Jesse ran a few dudes and a herd of Angus-Brahma cows at the foot of the mountains that are now part of the Bob Marshall wilderness. I got thrown in with a bunch of his hands and some of the locals when the whole community turned out to fight a range fire. The camp experience was more than I'd expected, and probably more than Dad had bargained for.

The only person near my age was a skinny kid named Cole. Cole lived in Great Falls, but had been left at the ranch for the summer when his parents returned to Great Falls. He was supposed to be "growing up" on the range, but I think they left him there to get rid of him. He needed a lot of growing. He was a smart-aleck, and clever and sneaky. He started out trying any trick he could think of to devil the older hands, but after one of them caught him and gave him a hiding with a bridle strap, he eased up and was almost human. Except with me. I had to be really careful to keep from walking into one of his tricks, most of which had painful results. I wasn't sure I could whip him, so I just did my best to keep out of his way.

The rest of the hands were a rough crew. I don't remember all their last names—maybe I never knew them—but their personalities stamped them in my memory forever. Jase had only one eye. The other, he said, had been ripped out by a grizzly. I think the "grizzly" was probably another old-timer he'd been drinking with who'd taken exception to Jase's lies. He sure could tell some good ones, and if he'd been everywhere he said he'd been and done everything he said he'd done, he'd have been over two hundred years old. Only thing is, after a while I learned that a good share of his lies were awful close to the truth.

The only hand dirtier and smellier than Jase was a nervous, skinny puncher named Tom. Tom, I swear, hadn't taken a bath since a steer knocked him off his horse while he was swimming a herd across the Marias River, and that had been eight years ago. It wasn't that he had anything against bathing. He just didn't figure he needed it. I can't vouch for the truth of this story, but Jase told me that Tom holed up in a line shack one winter and lived on beans and fatback. Along toward Christmas, a family of skunks moved out of their quarters under the shack looking for a place that didn't smell so bad.

The hands guessed Reb had come from Kentucky or Tennessee. Reb had been rousted out of his cabin way up in the mountains when the fire got near. He wore an old revolver, the only gun in the outfit, but he wore it all the time, even when he rolled up in his blanket at night. Reb always sat outside the firelight, with his back against a tree or a rock. It was considered bad manners to probe a man's past, and in Reb's case, it might have been downright dangerous. We guessed he thought maybe something or someone from his past might catch up with him. We just hoped we'd be out of the way if his suspicions ever came true.

The cook was a match for any of them. He was shiny bald except for a fringe of hair he let grow to his shoulders. Naturally, he was called Curly. Curly wore a big handlebar mustache and chewed tobacco, but that didn't give him enough kick, so he had a perpetual hand-rolled cigarette on his lip. The mustache dripped tobacco juice and the cigarette dribbled ashes so our grub was always well seasoned.

A ragged, skittish dog of multiple ancestry had taken to following the cook wagon, and Curly was no friend of dogs. Goddamned mutt, he called the dog. He kept after Jesse to get rid of it, but Jesse never did. I guess he thought it kept Curly on his toes.

Finally, old Curly got so fed up and cranky Cole told him we'd help him get rid of the dog. Cole got me in on his plan, at least part of it. Curly was cooking up a batch of doughnuts, so Cole rolled some of the dough into a cigar shape, rolled it in a burlap sack to make it look hairy, and cooked it dark. Looked just like something a dog had done. He tossed it under the table, and when the boys came in to eat, Curly pointed it out.

"Looky there whut that damn dog did. Crapped right here under the vittles. See? That's a dog turd."

"Naw, it ain't," someone said.

"Looks like one to me," I said. I picked up the doughnut and took a bite out of it. Some of the greener horns lost a lot of appetite right there.

"Yep, it's a dog tur—*&$%#*, it IS a dog turd." I spit and cussed and spit and puked and Cole laughed so hard he choked on his beans. I knew then who substituted the real thing. Even choking, Cole outran me. I came back to the cook wagon and grabbed a cleaver and was about to take out after Cole again when—

"Whoa!"

I recognized Reb's voice, and damn sure whoa'd.

"You don't want to do that," he said softly. "Sometimes what you do when you're mad follers you."

I guess right then I learned a lot more about old Reb. His eyes told me I'd better simmer down, so I dropped the cleaver and went off into the dark to sulk. And wait for Cole. But he didn't come back until daylight, and by then I'd gotten over most of my mad.

Back to the range fire, the reason we were gathered there. The year before, Jesse found himself with a string of yearling horses that he wanted to keep penned, but out of the way. Off in the mountains, he'd discovered a little valley almost completely circled with rocky cliffs. A small lake sat in the center of the valley, and a pretty decent meadow extended up toward the rocks. By blocking the trail out of the valley, he reckoned he could keep those yearlings there all summer. Grizzlies were really uncommon, and there was nothing else around to stampede them. With water and plenty of grass, this looked like horse heaven. Jesse drove the yearlings in, threw up a makeshift gate across the trail, and left them to fatten up until fall.

Winter snow came early and unexpectedly. A three-day blizzard covered the trail into the valley and piled up on the slopes above. When Jesse tried to move feed in to the horses, a couple of avalanches discouraged him so he waited for better weather.

Better weather came in late February.

When he finally got in to rescue those horses, Jesse carried a rifle in case any had survived and had to be shot. He was in for a surprise. The whole herd had survived,

81

although they looked like refugees from Buchenwald. Jesse is good at reading sign, and he was able to figure out what happened during the winter. When the snow fell, it gradually covered the meadow, so the horses moved farther up toward the surrounding rocks. Eventually, they pawed snow away all around the valley and there were not even roots to eat. They began nibbling the lichen on the rocks, and by the time the lichen ran out, they had developed a taste for rocks, so they had survived the winter on a little lichen and a lot of rocks. I sure wouldn't have wanted to judge their age that spring, the way their teeth were worn down. They were pretty weak until Jesse brought them hay and grain to strengthen them so he could drive them out to better pasture.

After we got the range fire out, I rode with Jesse when he set out to find what caused it. He tracked the fire back to the entrance of the little valley where the horses had wintered. By the way the fire had traveled, he was able to pinpoint just where it started. Tracks of shod horses crossed the trail at the fire origin, and he pointed out to me that a track should have showed right at the fire start. A steel horse shoe had struck a spark from a "horse apple" from one of those rock-eating horses and started a three-thousand-acre range and forest fire.

I carried one of those horse apples home to show Dad. He took it and struck it against a shovel and got sparks, all right, but he said he didn't believe those sparks were enough to start a range fire.

"Jesse's been known to stretch the truth once in a while. Musta been some cowpoke's cigarette," he said.

Well, I didn't argue with Dad. But I was with Jesse and we didn't see any cigarette up there.

Gold Mine

We called it The Hump. It's the mountain that stands between MacDonald Peak and the Valley. Most of the neighboring mountains extend above the tree line, but The Hump does not. The Hump had a special meaning in our lives. My mother used it as a weather gauge.

In my misspent youth, I carried cord after cord of wood for the two stoves in the farmhouse where I grew up. The kitchen range was used year-round, in fair weather and foul, whether the outside temperature was 40 below or 100 above. The other stove was "the heater," and it stood in what passed for a living room. During the winter the heater was supposed to keep the whole house warm, but when the a Montana winter really got going, the stove failed miserably to live up to its name. During the worst cold weather, we kept the door to the single bedroom closed, hoping to keep the two main rooms livable. Even so, if you were more than ten feet from a stove, you had a chance of being frostbitten. The bedroom, of course, got to be a little nippy, and my parents went to bed in long underwear and carrying hot water bottles. My domicile, the back porch, never saw heat. I slept under a horse blanket heavy enough to swayback a Percheron and carried flatirons wrapped in towels to bed with me.[5]

In the fall, Mother insisted that the heater be installed for the winter *only* after snow fell and *stayed* on The Hump, even when the weather was cool and we had frost. During a cold, dry fall, we clustered around the kitchen stove, hoping for snow, waiting for Mother to declare it time to put up the heater. In the spring when the snow went off The Hump, the heater came down, sometimes after couple of weeks of 80-degree weather, but more often just before a spell of 50-degree highs such as we always experienced in June.

Putting up the heater in the fall was a fairly easy task compared to taking it down in the spring. In the spring Dad might delay the task until a rainy day came, usually in mid-June. Mother covered the living room floor with newspapers before Dad disassembled the stovepipe. My job, from the time I was able to follow instructions, was to carry the sections of pipe outside without spilling soot on the floor. I might have had an easier job teaching pigs to fly. The winter's accumulation of soot filled the air and covered us, the newspapers on the floor, and any furniture that was exposed.

Once the pipe was outside, Dad wadded up a section of newspaper and stuffed it in the hole in the chimney. No, not to seal it. He lit the paper and burned the soot out of the chimney. THAT was the reason he had chosen a rainy day. The chimney spouted flame ten or twelve feet high much like a Bessemer furnace, and huge wads of burning soot wafted all around the house until the rain squelched them. Dad carried the heater to summer storage while Mother, amid much complaining about our carelessness,

---

[5]See "Sleeping in the Cold," *Building Character:Tales from Montana (And Other Damn Lies)* page 41.

cleaned up soot in the house for the rest of the day. By evening, only a thin film of soot lay on the table and the supper dishes.

Rumor has it that there is a gold mine somewhere on The Hump. Several people reported having found it once, but none had ever claimed to have gone back to it. One such discoverer was Dowd's older brother, Brutus, who advised us that the place was haunted and warned us away. Brutus' warning was enough for us.

Dowd, Murdie and I discussed the mine numerous times. Finally one summer we made plans to visit it and, perhaps, get rich. We pumped Brutus for information until he finally described the trail—a barely discernible mark. He informed us that rock slides blocked the trail on each side of the mine. "You can't miss it," he said, "it's between those two rock slides." We wondered why Brutus remembered more details every time we questioned him, and why he always stressed that the mine was haunted.

We included Rudy in our plans at the last minute, and were to regret that decision later. Rudy was from Philadelphia. He had been sent to visit an uncle for the summer, in order, we were sure, to keep him out of reform school. Rudy had many endearing habits. He smoked openly, while we sneaked an occasional cigarette. Rudy stole his uncle's beer and shared it with us. Rudy could cuss as well as, and sometimes better than, many of our fathers' friends. All in all, Rudy was an ideal companion for our thirteenth summer.

Another trait we liked in Ruddy was his gullibility. When it came to things on the farm and in the wild, Rudy was the greenest of greenhorns. We gathered cockleburs and set Rudy to incubating them, hoping to hatch baby porcupines. At first, we told him that skunks were quite tame and could be petted like cats, but then we agreed that was too cruel, even for Rudy, so we told him the truth. After the porcupine egg fiasco, he didn't believe us. We watched him constantly in the fields to make sure he never encountered a skunk. If he had, our source of beer might not have dried up but would have been too unpleasant to approach.

We didn't tell him cougar or grizzly bear stories—we expected to take him camping, and we saved such yarns for nights in the tent. When Rudy asked if he should take a gun along, we vetoed the idea. The thought of being in the mountains with a greenhorn carrying a gun scared even our normally indestructible souls. As it turned out, we were glad we had—for once—been wise.

We took stock at the trailhead. I had an oiled canvas for a tent, a hatchet, matches sealed in an empty shotgun shell, some bacon, some moldy smoked salmon and a box of crackers. Dowd carried a sleeping bag the size of a small cow, a frying pan, some dried soup and a canteen of water. Murdie brought blankets and a bag of potatoes.

Much, much later, we blamed the mosquitoes for all the trouble. Dowd and Murdie and I were accustomed to the mosquitoes, and suffered their bites in silence. Not city boy Rudy. He complained all the time, and well he might, because each bite swelled into a lump as big as half a peanut. In the shell. He had begged his uncle for mosquito netting after hearing from us about the insatiability of the mountain mosquitoes (in this case we told the truth), but the best he could do was some flimsy veil material his aunt had left over from a wedding dress. Besides his netting, Rudy had a five-pound sack of pancake flour, a quart of syrup and a pound of butter, as well as a tent complete with poles.

"No way can you carry all that, Rudy. Let's have some breakfast before we start," Dowd said. We started a fire and cooked half of Rudy's pancakes; and used all his syrup and all but a quarter pound of his butter.

The deer trail Dowd's brother described was easy to find, but not so easy to follow. It moved uphill or downhill in jumps that, for a deer, were probably an easy amble. It wandered along the mountainside in places so precipitous we were holding our breath. For three overloaded thirteen-year-olds it was a major undertaking.

We found a rock slide in the first half-mile, and we were sure we had to be near the mine. We climbed excitedly across the slide's shifting face, sending more rock to the jumble across the trail. Several times we thought we might add one or two of us to the pile. There was no mine on the far side of the slide. There wasn't enough room for a badger hole, let alone a mine entrance. Instead, we came upon another rock slide almost immediately. After the second and third and fourth rock slides, we were so hot and tired we were beginning to doubt Brutus' veracity and we were convinced the mine, had it ever really existed, was covered by a slide.

Darkness was falling and we were considering giving up and camping on the side of the mountain when we finally scrambled across a rock slide and found a pile of rocks out of place. And there was the mine. Spooky looking place. My hair follicles came to attention, and I know the other boys' did too because I could feel them, we were bunched so close together. Beyond the mine, the trail was clear ahead for as far as we could see in the dusk.

After a number of false starts, we set up Rudy's tent and then my canvas shelter. Rather than build a fire, we ate supper of crackers and moldy salmon while we discussed sleeping arrangements. No one volunteered to man the single tent. After some discussion of who was more scared than whom, we agreed that by scrunching together a little, we could all sleep in one tent.

Sometime in the night, I found myself sitting upright, along with three other jackknifed silhouettes.

"What's that?" came a whisper.

"OO-oo-oo-ooo-oo-oo," the sound that awakened us answered.

"G-g-g-ghost?"

"N-n-n-n-naw. N-n-no such thing. Wind in the t-t-trees," Dowd said.

We lay back and tried to sleep. The moan came again just as I was drifting off. I told myself Dowd was right; it was the wind. I didn't believe myself or Dowd either. Dowd, I saw, had his blanket pulled over his head. The sounds continued off and on all night, each time jerking me fully awake. Dawn finally came after several eons and a century or two.

In the bright morning sun the mine didn't seem spooky at all. After breakfasting on pancakes without syrup, we felt much bolder and more confident in our ability to cope with the wilds. We saved the leftover pancakes for lunch, covered them with Rudy's netting, and set out to find our fortune.

The old miner had either made a big enough strike to live well forever, or he'd given up too soon. The tunnel was so short that bright sunlight filtered in, and we could see, though dimly, all the way to the end. As we examined the solid rock face, we began to sweat and find the air oppressive. A hole in the ceiling told us the original owner may have had air trouble too and had built a ventilator, although we could see no light through the hole. Sensibly, we fled from the mine.

We felt better after we got back in the air. Having seen no sign of gold, we discussed whether to try again or to just go home. Murdie was determined to search for gold. Rudy voted for returning home, and accused us of lying about the mine all the time. Dowd and I were concerned about the air in the mine, and climbed up the hill above the stope to look for the ventilator outlet. We cleared away brush and gravel and sure enough, there it was. Soon we had it open enough so we thought the air might circulate. Just then, we looked down on the camp and saw camp robber jays after the leftover pancakes, our lunch-to-be. One of the jays caught up the netting with his pancake haul and flew right toward the mine. Without thinking, I shouted, "Get out of there! That's mine."

Murdie came barreling out of the stope. He ran right over poor Rudy who had dropped to his knees with his hands clasped and his eyes closed. Rudy got up and followed Murdie—for about twenty-five yards—then passed him like a shot. Dowd and I hurried down the slope and intercepted Rudy, fearing he might get lost if he went far. We had to tackle him and hold him while he kept saying, "Ghost! Ghost!"

Murdie stopped when the jay overtook him and he saw what the "ghost" was. Sheepishly, he joined us.

When we sorted things out, Dowd and I thought the sight of Murdie and Rudy racing down the trail was about the funniest thing that ever happened. Murdie eventually could smile a bit, too. Not Rudy. He swore vengeance, and we knew he meant it. We were glad he hadn't brought a gun. When Rudy hiked away down the trail without looking back, the three of us came down with a bad case of scruples. We knew we couldn't leave a city boy alone in the mountains, so we had to go after him. We spent the next day practically dragging him back to civilization.

We never went back to the mine. Maybe it wasn't haunted, but it sure was bad luck.

The Pheasant Problem

The lower Flathead Valley teemed with ring-necked pheasants when I was in my teens. We called them Chinese Pheasants, or, more often, chinks. Even though they were everywhere, they were seldom a problem. Oh, some soreheads complained when pheasants ate a little grain in the fall, not taking into account the pounds and pounds of insects a single pheasant consumed during the summer. Once in a while a nesting hen pheasant got

90

caught up in our combine and jammed the works. Chewed-up pheasant is hell to get out of a combine cylinder. And in hunting season, we were overrun with dudes who left gates open and hunted right among the stock.

Old Tom Pleasant was unusual in a town full of truthful people. He was known for his frequent misrepresentation of the truth. In fact, Tom was sometimes called a bald-faced liar, even though he wore a full beard. Tom took no offense, just chuckled and looked like a kid caught in the cookie jar, even if we accused him of lying when the story he told was the honest-to-God truth.

When Old Tom started raising chickens, he began to come up with the damnedest tales about his chickens and the varmints that were after them. He complained about finding coyotes digging under the pens and having to run out half a dozen times to pull a coyote out by the tail just as it got almost inside. We knew that one was a lie. When you pull a coyote out like that, he'll turn and bite you. You pull on the hind legs so he can't reach back to you. I never saw any tooth marks on Old Tom's arms.

Tom told about the bobcat that got into his hen house and caused such a commotion that Tom went out with his shotgun. He aimed at the cat, but the cat moved and Tom killed his best rooster, besides blowing a hole in the side of the chicken house. We hadn't heard of a bobcat down on the flat where Tom lived for twenty years or more, so when he showed us the "bobcat," we weren't surprised to see that it was one of Tom's wife's housecats.

When he told us that the ring-necked pheasants were giving him a hard time, we wondered what kind of a yarn he'd make up about that. But that's all he said—he was having a hell of a time with the damn pheasants. I was curious. I liked to hear his lies (being an apprentice liar

91

myself) and really looked forward to the tale. Every time I pestered him to tell me, he clammed up and walked away, until one day he'd had enough and told me to come by his place and he'd show me.

Happened that I was out that way a day or two later, and I stopped by. Tom was grouchy as a grizzly with the gout, but he took me out to his barnyard where the chickens ran free. His old rooster looked frazzled and worried as a chicken can look, and was jumpy as a grasshopper on a skillet. Then I saw why—Old Tom hadn't been lying. I caught a glimpse of movement near the barn, and saw one of those gaudy cock pheasants sneaking around. The rooster saw him too, and took after him. While he chased that pheasant, another came in and tupped two hens right before our eyes. The rooster came charging back, and the first pheasant was onto a hen before the rooster could turn around.

"See what I mean?" Tom asked.

"Well, what harm can that do?"

"What harm? Look at these eggs. Half of them are the size of pheasant eggs. And the hens have found out that those are easier on their arses, and of course the damn fools are seduced by the pretty feathers and they've got so they welcome the goddam pheasants."

He did have a point. I helped him gather his eggs, and damned of we didn't have to pick up nineteen eggs before we had a dozen.

Fishin' Worms

It all began when we cleaned the chicken house. In the summer, our chickens (Mother insisted they were *her* chickens) ran free to scavenge around the farm. Oh, they were fed grain once or twice a day, but they supplemented our feeding with grasshoppers, earthworms, garden seed, cutworms, leavings where we threw the slop bucket, and other delicious tidbits, including the green and brown flies that used cowpies for a nursery. Nowadays, such chickens sell as "free range" chickens, and command a hefty bonus on the market. I guess they taste better. Maybe it's the green and brown flies. Maybe it's the slop-bucket leavings.

For those moderns who have never lived through it, I'd better explain the slop bucket (not to be confused with a slop *jar*). Having no garbage disposal, indeed, no sewer and no garbage collection as such, we used a large pail to collect odds and ends of scraps, dishwater, and such. Over years of use, this pail collected a black patina which thickened with age.

Dad caught H.B. cleaning his slop bucket one day.

"Don't do it," Dad advised.

"How come?"

"I scoured ours out and when I got to the bottom, there wasn't any bottom there. It had rusted clean away years ago."

When the slop bucket got full, it was my unpleasant duty to empty it. Usually I dumped it in an area behind the outhouse, or I did until that area out-stank the privy. Then we chose another place for this discharge, as it were. The scraps made dessert pickings for the chickens, but the soil became too sour for the propagation of fishin' worms.

Came fall and frosty toes, the egg output dropped, so the chickens were confined to the chicken house until March or April when they could again roam free without suffering chilblains.

The chicken house was a rickety shed in which Dad had installed some unpeeled pine poles for roosts and straw-filled apple boxes for nests. Despite its somewhat Spartan interior, the chickens seemed to appreciate it, especially when the temperature hung down below zero for a week or two, and their water froze and had to be replaced with warm water two or three times a day.

Come spring, the chickens were freed to forage. They had become attached to the chicken house, so they returned every night. At least, most of them did. One of my chores from the time I was nine or ten was to lock the chicken house against the marauding coyotes, weasels, skunks and other predators Mother imagined in the night.

As soon as the chickens were "let out" in the spring, Mother began her campaign to have the chicken house cleaned. All winter long the chickens had prospered, the only concession to their comfort being an occasional addition to the straw on the floor, but now she declared the chicken house an unhealthy place that would cause sickness among her chickens.

Farming entails many unpleasant tasks, and cleaning the chicken house is not the least onerous. Think about it. Chickens are birds, much like large pigeons, and anyone can see the effect of having pigeons around. Imagine a hundred or so pigeons confined for the entire Montana winter, multiply their droppings by four, and you're close to imagining a chicken house. Besides the droppings, chickens have mites, and whenever we stirred the dust around, I imagined that the dust was full of mites. Just the thought made me itch. Still does.

Dad was a Master Dreader. When a job he particularly disliked came along, he'd say, "Wait. I gotta dread that a while first." I learned to dread from his fine example. Cleaning the chicken house came high on the list of distasteful farm chores to dread. A person shouldn't tackle a chore like that without the proper amount of dreading because, if he hadn't dreaded long enough, he might find he'd finished the job without being prepared to enjoy the associated misery properly.

Cleaning the chicken house was one of those jobs so unpleasant we would rather have cleaned the outhouse. Well, no. It wasn't *that* unpleasant, I guess. At any rate, Mother nagged, Dad and I dreaded, and the chickens roamed free in the spring sun.

Finally there came a day when Dad couldn't find a good excuse, and teasing Mother about her poor little sickly chickens (any one of which could have bested a boa in a wrestling match) paled to the point where he decided it was time to clean the #@#&%*# chicken house. Funny, this always occurred on Saturday, and when I mentioned this to Dad, he just said he didn't want be the only one having all the fun.

Dad had built a sloping plane under the roosts with one-by-two slats at intervals. I suppose this was built so that, if a hen decided she didn't want to make the trip to a laying box, her egg would not fall or roll all the way to the floor. I hated that ramp. Throughout the year, dissident hens chose to lay their eggs in corners under the ramp, and I was the one chosen to crawl in there to gather eggs. When it came time to clean up, I was also the "volunteer" who scraped manure and feathers (and mites) in that enclosed space. If I had dared use some of Dad's words, I might have sanitized the area; but, then again, I probably would have caused a dust explosion.

We dumped the chicken-house residue in a pile next to the garden. Chicken manure is high in nitrogen—so high that it is too strong to be used as fertilizer until it's had some time to decompose. The pile never decomposed to the point at which Dad thought it could be spread with the manure spreader so it sat and stank.

Fishin' worms loved the ground around the manure pile, and prospered fantastically. We dug worms out a couple of feet from the pile, and they were ideal for catching catfish. Bullheads. Mud cats, some called them. As we dug closer and closer to the pile, the worms we found were larger and larger. Right at the edge of the pile, we found worms as big as our fingers, and downright aggressive. When some of Mother's baby chicks disappeared, Dad and I were careful not to tell her about the big worms. That was probably where the chicks went, and, if Mother found out, we'd be out there destroying worms. NOTHING must harm her chickens.

These big worms were too tough (their hides *and* their dispositions) to get a hook into, so we tied them to the hook. Turned out we didn't need a hook. When the fish grabbed one of those worms, the worm took exception and grabbed back. The worm coiled around the fish, and when we recognized that something was going on at the end of the line, we pulled out fish and worm. No need to get the hook out of the fish, but unwrapping an angry worm from a fish was no easy job, either.

Then along came Big Oscar. One day when we were digging worms, he must have been curious, for he crawled out of the very center of the pile of chicken manure It took Dad and me together to subdue him. He[6] was the grandpappy of all fishin' worms. The Oscar Meyer wiener wasn't famous yet, but Oscar, while retracted, could have modeled for a whole package of those wieners. Fully extended, he was twenty-seven and eleven-sixteenths inches long. Tying Oscar to a hook would have been a travesty, so I made a sort of angleworm harness. Oscar bucked and strained against the harness like any Cayuse, and tried to wrap around my neck to strangle me, but I finally got him harness broke, and took him fishing. Before I dropped him in deep to get down to real business, I dipped him a few times until he got the idea and took a deep, deep breath, gave me a thumbs up, and dived in to test the fish. He took to fishing like the proverbial duck to water. His attitude was, "Let me at 'em," and he'd spit on his hands (well, no, he didn't exactly have hands, but you know what I mean) and eagerly dive in looking for fish.

Because of Oscar, I gained fame and glory as an expert fisherman. I caught the biggest bass ever landed from Kicking Horse Reservoir. I caught twenty-inch trout where most people caught eight and nine-inchers. I caught three

---

[6] Yes, I know. Angleworms are neither *he* nor *she*, but are hermaphrodites, therefore both. Oscar's personality was such that I declared him a *he*.

and four perch at a cast. I wanted to take Oscar ice fishing—there were some really big fish out there under the ice. When I suggested winter fishing to him, though, he looked at me like I was nuts and hurried, shivering, deep into his lair.

Between fishing expeditions, I fed Oscar whatever I could find that he liked. He was partial to coffee grounds, fermented tomatoes and Copenhagen snuff; but for a rotten egg, he'd come out of his hole sit up like a dog to beg. His breath, of course, was something else.

I fished with Oscar for two years before tragedy struck. Somehow, a rattlesnake made its way onto the farm and Oscar took one look and fell in love. We never knew whether Oscar's male end or female end fell for the snake—I'm no authority on the sexing of snakes—but Oscar, being who he was, didn't care.

His affection was not reciprocated. The snake simply turned his (her? its?) back and crawled away. Oscar, of course, was devastated. He sulked in his hole and refused to come out even for his favorite chew of snoose. I searched and searched for a rotten egg, and finally found some unhatched pheasant eggs, but even these didn't coax him out.

Time went on, and finally, on a late summer day, Oscar crept out of his hole. He was not the same. He seemed to have contracted rheumatism, and his joints were so stiff he looked like a string of Crazy Ikes when he crawled. We saw him a few more times during the fall, but when the snow went off the next year, he didn't appear. We assumed he'd passed quietly away during the winter under the pile of chicken manure, so, out of respect for Oscar, we left it be. Years later, when I left the farm, the pile was still there, a memorial to the greatest fishin' worm of all time.

Charlie

I suppose everyone has a nickname or two, but when I was young, I went through nicknames faster than I went through shoes. When I was very small, Mother started to call me "Bill"; but when some of Dad's cousins spoke of me as "Willie" once or twice, Mother blew her top. (It was fortunate that Mother's top was hinged, so she could blow it without real harm.) She declared that I was "Richard" from then on. My teachers acquiesced and called me Richard throughout my grade-school years, and only with great argument and effort did I become "Dick" in high school. I told you the real reason before.[7]

I always had some other nickname, though. For a time I was "Stinker."[8] My best friends, Dowd and Murdie, called me "Chicken" most of the time. I haven't the faintest idea why. Dad called me "Runt" most of the time, a name that fit particularly well because I was always small for my age. (I'd still be small for my age, if everything I eat didn't go to my waist.) Later on, to distinguish me from another Dick, I was called "Lucky", an inappropriate name if ever there was one.

Sometime in the 1930s, a New Deal-sponsored series of entertainment programs came to the small towns in Montana. Called Northwest Assemblies, the series was, I think, the WPA of vaudeville players, although, at the time, vaudeville was terminally ill and probably on its deathbed.

In small towns like Charlo, the programs were held in the school gymnasium. The cost was something like a

---

[7]See "Why William is Called Dick," *More Montana: Tall Tales, Damn Lies and Otherwise* page 48.
[8]See "Stinker," *Building Character:Tales from Montana (And Other Damn Lies)* page 1.

dime per person, about all anyone could afford. I remember one pair of comedians whose act went like this:

"What's your name, son?"

"Potts. Phil Potts." Some titters from the audience.

"Phil Potts. Hmm. Do you have any brothers and sisters?"

"Yes, I have a sister, Carrie."

"Phil Potts and Carrie Potts." The audience is snickering, now. This is pretty racy stuff for 1933.

"Who's your father?"

"My dad's M. T. Potts."

"Hmm. Phil Potts, Carrie Potts and M. T. Potts." The rube audience is in stitches, because on the farm we all did all of those but we didn't mention them in polite society. Well, such material may not have killed vaudeville, but probably gave it a terrible bellyache.

At any rate, one of the ventriloquist acts that came through was called "Charlie and Cal." I forget whether Charlie was the dummy or the ventriloquist of the comedy team, but I considered his jokes the funniest I had ever heard in my tender years. I repeated them over and over and added a few corny ones of my own. My long-suffering parents asked me, "Who do you think you are, Charlie?" I must have said yes, because my parents, particularly my mother, began to call me "Charlie." When she was in a good humor. When she was in a bad humor, I was still Richard. I don't think she ever called me Dick. Until she died, her pet name for me was Charlie.

Marta

She was different from our usual run of cows. Most of them were gentle and easily cowed. Not Marta. She had her own ways about things and one horn to enforce them. Dad often said he was going to remove that one horn. What he actually said was, "I'm gonna dehorn that dirty old #%%*^* one of these days."

He gave me, who weighed somewhere near ninety pounds, the job of catching Marta, which shows either his lack of judgment or his sense of humor. I suspect it was the latter.

"Catch her up and snub a halter on her. You know how to do that. Just run a loop under the rope and over her nose. Haltered, she's gentle as a lamb."

Ha.

I managed to throw a noose over Marta's head after the third try. I had to throw when she raised her head from cropping grass, which wasn't often.

When she noticed the rope around her neck, she decided to go elsewhere. She started off at a slow walk, and I tried to turn her. No luck. Dad had told me to hold onto that rope after I caught her, so I held onto the rope. I dug in my heels to hold her, and I might as well have tried to hold a Sherman tank. She kept walking. When I tripped and fell, it signaled her to begin to trot. I got to my feet and trotted after her, necessarily, since I still held the rope. When I tripped the next time, Marta went into a gallop. She dragged me through thistles and the standard set of cowpies, then through ditches to wash me off, then through the mud at the edge of the pothole, and back through the ditch.

Finally, fat old Marta got winded and stopped. I walked up to her, confident that I could halter her now. That was when she noticed how small her adversary was. She turned around, put her head down, and charged me. Even Dad ducked out of the way when Marta got her dander up. He'd go for a club and settle her down. I had no club, so I took off running. I still held the rope.

A single volunteer cottonwood tree grew in the back pasture. It was only a few years old, but was strong enough to hold me. Despite the lack of lower branches, I hiked myself up that tree. Marta, incensed, decided to climb the tree too. She had left her climbers at the barn, or I swear she'd have gotten me. As it was, she stood on her hind legs and pawed at the tree. This was my chance. I tied the rope to one of the high limbs. Now, I thought, if she backs down, she'll hang herself.

Huh-uh.

Marta dropped to all fours, and the spindly tree-top bent under her weight, throwing me from the tree. Marta tried to catch me, but the tree played her like a fish on a line. She couldn't get to me, and I couldn't get her free. Try as I might, I couldn't get back up that tree without a mad cow behind me.

I turned to look for help from Dad, but could see he was of no use. When a person has to hug a fence post to keep from falling over laughing, he isn't going to be much help roping cattle. I sat down out of Marta's reach and sulked. Marta raged around a while, then went over to the tree and lay down in the meager shade. The taut rope held her head up but didn't seem to bother her much. I crept around to her blind side, and shinnied up the tree. I yelled at her, and she stood up. The change in tension on the rope almost shook me from the tree. Seeing me in the tree reminded her of her anger, and she again tried to climb the tree. I untied the slackened rope and let it drop to the ground. As far as I was concerned, the damn cow was roped and my job was finished.

Dad released his fence post and strolled over. His comment was his usual.

"Are ya havin' any fun?"

Marta dropped to the ground and looked at him suspiciously. Before she could decide to attack, Dad walked up to her head, haltered her and led her away.

"You've had your fun up in that tree. You can come down now," he called back to me.

After that, I begged him to dehorn the "dirty old #%%*^*" for sure. He didn't.

"Anything that's that much fun to have around I won't mess with," he said.

Raging Bulldog

"Daddy said you upset his bees."

"But I didn't—" but Sarah Beth walked away, holding her books tight to her chest. Her expression was the one she might have had were she smelling bad cheese. From my crumbling world, I wished she'd let me tell her my story.

Potholes dotted the lower Flathead Valley when I was growing up, each pond having beside it a mound of dirt. The larger the mound, the deeper the pond. Farmers have since filled many of the potholes to increase their irrigatable acreage, but one can still see a few potholes with their dirt mounds as you drive along Highway 93. Scientists, who think they know everything, maintain that these potholes were formed at the end of the last ice age. As the lake drained, they say, icebergs ran aground in the shallow water and wind and wave motion caused enough movement so that the icebergs wallowed out the ponds, leaving the mounds of dirt beside them.

Baloney.

Anyone familiar with the real history realizes that this is another batch of scientific male cow droppings. The truth is, Paul Bunyan wintered the Blue Ox in the Flathead one year, and the potholes and mounds are Babe's tracks and the mud squished up from them.

Our farm shared a fairly large pothole with our neighbors. The common fence across this pond was the one I was repairing when the wire I was holding broke, requiring the application of my father's Peerless tobacco poultices to each hand.

We also shared the mound of dirt (we called it a hill) beside the pond. To be equitable, we had most of the pond; the neighbor had most of the mound. His side was high and dry enough that the local beekeeper maintained six or eight hives of bees thereon. When I wandered to the far end of our farm, I usually had to pass the pothole so, being too lazy to detour around the pond, I crossed the fence and walked past the beehives. I believe bees get to know a person, and realize who is or is not a threat. Either that or I was just dumb. At any rate, by summer's end I walked among the beehives with impunity, though not with my friends. This was one place where I out-gutted them.

One year, this neighboring farm was rented to a scruffy character who owned a small herd of scruffy cattle. He also owned a scrub Jersey bull, whose name, we learned, was Elmer. Jerseys aren't very big, and Elmer was small even for his breed. He might have been little for big, but he was hell for bad humor and belligerence. Most of the bulls in the neighborhood were either friendly or could be cowed, so to speak, with a stick and a loud voice. Not this one. Not Elmer.

When I walked along the line fence, Elmer trotted over and snorted at me, wishing he could get through the fence at me. Consequently, when I took the shortcut through the beehives, I made sure Elmer wasn't in the vicinity. Except once.

My little bulldog, Snooks, followed me (or perhaps led me) everywhere. On the day of my memory lapse, she shied away from the beehives while I walked casually through them. I was paying attention only to my own thoughts—bees made me think of the beautiful Sarah Beth—when I heard a snort and the sound of trotting hooves. I knew I'd lose a race to the fence, and the pond wasn't deep enough to protect me. I was at Elmer's mercy.

Then Snooks remembered she was a bulldog. She intercepted Elmer's charge, and stood yapping at him. He tried to gore her, but she dodged adroitly. Then she seized his tender nose, and held on, (may I say it?) doggedly. Elmer shook his head, but Snooks held on. Elmer tried to drag her under his front feet, but she was smart and agile and would have none of that. Elmer bawled his surrender, but Snooks knew she had the world by the tail, and was not inclined to let go.

Then, Elmer's gyrations smashed Snooks against a beehive and Snooks shook loose, taking a hefty chunk of bull nose with her. I caught her up and dashed to the pond and into the water. I knew what was coming: bees.

Elmer was not out of the woods by any means. The bees flew out *en masse* to investigate the commotion and found a panting, nose-bleeding Elmer the only target. They set to work with a will. They sought the places with the least hair covering, around his face and between his legs where his maleness hung.

His eyes covered with stinging bees, Elmer went berserk. He rubbed his head on the ground, and thrashed about, upsetting another hive and doubling the number of tormentors. Finally he gathered his wits, if he had any, and galloped away for the farthest side of the field. The cloud of bees followed for a while, then flowed back toward the hives.

Snooks and I lay low in the water, finally swimming through the fence to the far side of the pond.

For the rest of the summer, I detoured far around the beehives. And the beekeeper. Dating his beautiful daughter was one of my greatest ambitions, but he somehow learned about my small part in the hive destruction, and looked with disfavor on my suit and any ties I wished to establish.

Alas for the dreams of youth.

Snow Snakes

The folks up in Alaska report that they have ice worms during the really cold winter. I'm not sure whether ice worms actually exist, since some Alaskans are inclined to exaggerate a bit; but I am sure that there is a similar phenomenon here in the Pacific Northwest.

Most residents of the northern tier of states are aware that snow snakes exist here. I suppose a few folks in the southern states have heard of them, and probably wondered if they were real. (I suspect that, when they read reports of the winter temperatures, some of those southern people wonder if the northern tier itself is real.)

Just as the trees need prolonged warm weather before they put out leaves, snow snakes need a blanket of snow and prolonged especially cold weather—at least five degrees below zero—for several days before they make their appearance. When we have a dry winter with little snow, or if a thaw precedes the cold snap, we may have no snow snakes at all that year.

Snow snakes are white and appear only when there is sufficient snow to camouflage them. The they are so well hidden that few people have actually seen them. Even unseen, the snow snake can be extremely dangerous. Many a skier has taken an unexpected and unexplained fall when a snow snake became wrapped around a ski. Experienced skiers watch the weather, and will avoid snake-infested slopes after a below-zero cold snap.

It's fortunate that the snakes are so well hidden. They are poisonous, but if you can't see them and don't know you've been bitten, the poison does not affect you. The only person who I'm sure saw the snow snake that bit him was the town drunk. He managed to fight off the poison with a bottle of cheap whiskey.

107

Bear Wrangler

Old Bill Kittmeister[9] said I wasn't worth a damn as a roper. He hurt my feelings, but in my heart I knew he was right. Nevertheless, when the local rodeo planned a bear roping, I was quick to sign up for the contest. I didn't know what I was getting into.

The day before the rodeo, I borrowed a well-seasoned cow pony, with the idea that roping a bear is a lot like roping a cow. Boy, was I wrong.

Normally, the rodeo grounds, like any good corral, were surrounded by pole fences that made for easy climbing for a fallen rider. More containment was needed for a bear roping, and the arena was fenced differently. Eight-foot boards set on end formed two sides. The barns and chutes for holding the rodeo stock formed one side, and the grandstand, raised six feet to provide some fence, faced the open side.

Came time for the bear roping, we ropers paraded into the arena, and a wagon backed out of the barn. A box on the wagon opened and dumped the bear out. Several of the horses, when they saw and scented the bear, put on a finer show of bucking than the regular broncs.

The group of ropers was halved very soon, and some of those still on horseback were in no position to throw a rope. My borrowed horse shied a little, then settled down, although he was a bit nervous. The bear, unceremoniously chucked into the ring, looked around and found himself surrounded. He took a look at the riders and the mass of enemies in the stands and decided that any way out was a good way. He loped over to one of the fences. His claws

---

[9]See "Lady," *Building Character:Tales from Montana (And Other Damn Lies)* page 120.

couldn't get sufficient hold to get him up the eight feet, but to give him credit, he kept trying, throwing splinters right and left.

While he was occupied, I rode in close and threw my loop. Best throw I ever made. When the rope tightened, the horse stopped as he was trained. The bear came to his end of the rope and turned around. I guess he decided my horse was the cause of all the noise and indignity, so after him he came.

The horse took one look at the bear charging toward him, gave a high, desperate whistle and took off in the other direction, which happened to be toward the grandstand, while I grabbed all the leather I could lay my hands on. I sure didn't want to be left behind with a bear.

That old horse jumped the measly six-foot fence like a thoroughbred and galloped up the steps of the grandstand. The bear scrambled over the fence after him and the audience scattered like quail.

Somewhere along the line, the bear and the horse ran past opposite sides of a post, and shortly the rope jerked taut. Bear, horse and rider came down in a tumble.

Just about that time, someone with the only presence of mind in the whole arena cut the rope with an ax. The bear popped out of the heap and took off for the tall timber. The horse scrambled up, stood there trembling and committed an indiscretion of major proportions on the grandstand seats. I led him back to the arena and to the barn to clean up the cuts and scrapes. There were surprisingly few on the horse, but many and major on the rider.

And that's the last time I signed up for a bear roping.

The Topers

Farmers in the Flathead, at one time, raised hundreds of acres of sugar beets, and fed beet pulp to their livestock. Beet pulp, in case you wonder, is the fibrous part of the sugar beet left after the sweet juice is squeezed out. After the stuff lay around for a while, it fermented. Cows loved it. Some of them may have been alcoholics, but none of our cows were. After Dad fed pulp to our cows and pigs and they got drunk, Mother put her Methodist foot down and forbade the stuff on our farm.

Ensilage also ferments, especially if it's made from green and sugary fodder. We didn't feed it, but Dowd's family did, and I was spectator to some great cow orgies.

Seeing a drunken cow or pig ought to be enough to make a man stop drinking. I don't know of any case in which it *did*, but it ought to. Like human drunks, some cows got a load of alcoholic courage and went on the prod, butting other cows around and sometimes becoming belligerent enough to challenge the boss cow. Others romped around like boisterous young calves. Still others, except for their glassy eyes, looked sober as an owl. There were those who looked for all the world like drunks crying in their beer, and those who just lay down and took a nap.

Drunken pigs raced around fighting and squealing until the alcohol began to wear off, then lay down in the shade to nurse their hangovers. (A word of caution. Don't go into the pen with a large sow if she's hung over.)

Dowd and I sought to exploit the "still" in the silo. We buried a jug at the base of the silo near one of the doors, and extracted it in the spring when the ensilage was ripe. That stuff was awful. We had to hold our noses to drink it. Seeing drunken cows didn't make me quit drinking, but those corn squeezings *almost* did.

The Weasel

Adult gophers drove the young away from the nest about the middle of July. Those mere babies scattered about the farm, and almost every year one or two passed through our outbuildings. The old hens, spying the small animal, gave the alarm.

"Weasel! Danger! Fly! Help! Squa-a-a-ak!"

The poor baby gopher wondered what the excitement was, until Snooks arrived. Then the gopher was in deadly danger. He'd head for the woodpile. Snooks then recruited me to dismantle the woodpile so she could rid the farm of the deadly menace. If the wood was ricked up, I poked with a broom handle between the sticks and routed the gopher that way. If the wood was just dumped in a disorderly pile, I moved one block at a time until I got close to the little varmint, at which time he/she ducked quickly to another space between blocks. Sometimes I scattered the blocks all over the woodlot before Snooks could do her duty. I'm not sure, but I guess this was fun.

When the weasel showed up, the story took a different turn. The weasel didn't cooperate and go to ground in the woodpile. Instead it hid in impossibly small holes under boards in the barn lot.

Mother sometimes had a few bantam chickens around. They weren't good for much. They were too small to make good eating, and were tough besides, and their eggs were hardly one bite. I suspect Mother liked them because they were much like her—small, feisty survivors. The bantam rooster wasn't afraid of anything as long as it was daylight; and, high in the trees where he roosted, he wasn't afraid of much of anything at night, either. The weasel fazed him not a bit, and we could tell where it was by the rooster's actions.

When I moved the boards, the weasel sped like a flash to another hiding place, eventually taking refuge in an old cream separator. In this cast-iron tunnel, it should have been safe. Snooks couldn't get in, and I knew better than to reach in there. If I poked a stick at it, the weasel just dodged, chattering at me angrily all the time. I left Snooks in charge and got out my .22.

Kids, don't try this at home. Adults, don't try this *anywhere.*

I aimed at the weasel in the separator and fired. The echo of the gunshot deafened me and sent Snooks to watching from twenty feet away. Pieces of ricocheting bullet came out of the opening in a spray, and I was fortunate that none of them hit a vital part, although one bit of lead lodged in my neck and remained there for years. I looked in the separator and the weasel was unharmed. Weasels are fast. I had tried shooting one at the entrance to a gopher hole, and I could see where the bullet struck the dirt—exactly where the weasel's head had been. I was convinced that he, like Superman, was faster than a speeding bullet.

I'd had enough of this weasel. I wasn't strong enough to lift the separator, but I did it anyway and dumped the weasel out. He and Snooks fought around the barnyard for several minutes. Snooks grabbed, the weasel bit back. Snooks yelled, releasing the weasel, and the fight began again in a new location. Size and strength overcame at last, and Snooks came to me for praise and treatment of her numerous weasel cuts. I treated her but I hid my own wound from Mother.

And I never, ever told Dad about this. He thought I was responsible with guns.

Flashing Firewood

I was seldom able to put one over on Dad. He seemed to have a sixth sense about my indiscretions. When I asked H.B. if I should tell Dad I smoked, he said, "Aw, your daddy knows you smoke." When beer was brought to the hayfield and I asked for some, Dad said, "Go ahead and try it. You might not like it. Now if it was wine..." At the time, I went to town on Tuesday night and a friend and I shared a bottle of wine, got puking drunk, and, by drinking lots of water for the next few days, stayed high until Friday.

I pulled off one shenanigan without Dad's getting wise, though.

The farm next to us was a rental, owned by Eneas Conko who lived up in the foothills. Over the years, we had neighbors of every kind there: good ones, like Jess Wilson, and no-accounts like Orville. Orville had a speech impediment—in those days, we said he was tongue-tied—and his name, as he pronounced it, was Orble. Orble avoided both work and soap, and was short on respect for property ownership. He borrowed any tool he could, sometimes without asking, and when questioned about it, swore he'd brought it back. After Orble had collected a goodly number of tools and whatnot, Dad would make a social call and manage to drift into the shed where Orville kept his "borrowed" tools.

"While I'm here," Dad would say, "I think I'll be needing these." And he'd pick up an armful of tools to carry home. Orville never tried to claim ownership, so the ploy worked time after time. When Dad told H.B. about his ruse, H.B. knocked out his pipe before he spoke.

"Well, I just don't loan my tools out," he said, hinting that Dad was a damn fool for doing so. In fact, Dad often described himself that way when he needed a tool that Orville had borrowed.

In my teens I was the chief wood splitter and bringer-inner. We sawed the logs into lengths that fit the cook stove, and then the fun began. The lower sections of a large pine or fir split easily, but sometimes the log had many, many knots in it, and splitting enough to fill the wood box was back-breaking work. Generally, by the time I split a day's worth of kitchen wood, the air around the woodlot had a faint aura of azure. The air would have been purple if I had dared use Dad's words.

One year, Dad brought home a whole bull pine tree. Such a tree tends to be knotty near the top, but this one had grown in the open and had big knots from top to bottom. Splitting that wood was a mighty tough chore.

When some of the split, ready-for-cook-stove wood turned up missing, I supposed my mother and sister were helping carry wood into the house. I thanked them, but both denied it, pointing to the unfilled wood box. When I found man tracks in the snow on the side of the woodpile nearest to Orville's shack, I was more than a little suspicious. I kept watch, and whenever the pile went down unexpectedly, more tracks appeared, always leading toward Orville's. Enough was enough. I wasn't about to split wood for that no-good S.O.B.

I spent most of a Sunday afternoon setting my trap. I bored holes a few inches deep into a half-dozen sticks of stove wood, emptied the powder from three or four shotgun shells into each opening, and carefully carved a plug for each hole. When I was finished it was hard to see that the sticks had been tampered with; but, to make doubly sure, I dipped the doctored ends in mud. I stacked this wood along with some legitimate sticks at the end of the pile where Orville had been scavenging. I instructed my mother and sister not to use that wood, but they told me (nastily) to shut up and keep the wood box filled, and that they had no intention of disturbing my precious woodpile.

I kept an eye on the woodpile, and a few days later noticed some more wood was missing, including some of my marked sticks. I didn't have long to wait for results. Next morning, I woke to what seemed to be some really artistic cussing, although it was so garbled I couldn't make out the exact words. I jumped into my icy clothes and went out to see what was going on. Dad was trying to calm down a choleric Orble.

"I think he says I tried to kill him," Dad said.

"How's that?" I asked innocently, forcing myself not to smile at Orble's soot-stained face and clothing.

"Near as I can tell, he says our wood blew up in his stove."

I could no more refrain from asking than I could refrain from breathing.

"What the heck was our wood doing in his stove?"

My, it was hard keeping a straight face. Dad caught on then.

"Yeah, Orville, what's this about our wood in your stove? We don't give wood away."

Orville suddenly found that he'd cut the ground from under himself. He shut up and stomped away toward his shack.

I still held my laughter, wondering what Dad would say, now that my little trick had come out and proved dangerous. About that time I heard a snicker from around the corner of the house.

"Dad blame me," H.B. said. "I had to run like the dickens to get here to see that."

I was still holding my laughter, waiting for a clue from Dad.

"I heard this bang," H.B. said, "and I looked over there at Orville's and there was smoke and soot coming out of the window and the door and the chimney, and when Orville came out he looked just like another cloud of soot. When he started to hot-foot it over here, I reckoned there'd be some entertainment in it."

At that he started to laugh out loud, and I broke down completely. My trap had worked better than I had expected. Dad, being outnumbered, began to laugh too.

Later, when H.B. had wiped off his tears and gone home, Dad did manage, between chuckles, to warn me not to do such a thing again. He didn't have to. Orville moved away the next day.

Army Cot?

Old Oliver Tweep
Takes walks in his sleep
And wanders around in the dark.
One day he was found
Passed out on the ground
Of Soldiers' Memorial Park.

Combining

The old threshing rigs that used to travel around began to fade out in the 1930s; they have been replaced by the combine, which, as its name implied, combined the functions of the "header" or "binder" and the big threshing machine. The combine eliminated the manual labor of shocking bundles and then pitching them onto a wagon and hauling them to the maw of the big threshing rig. The combine operator charged by the acre, more or less depending on the qualities of the field. Weedy fields, hills, extra-heavy crops cost more.

About 1940, Dad and H.B. wondered if they could save money by buying a small combine together and doing their own work. The major event that decided them was the rainstorm that blew down much of their heaviest-producing grain. The big combines that worked the area weren't able to pick up the downed grain, and Dad and H.B. lost considerable crop. "Crop" translated from farmerese means "money." So they bought a small John Deere machine.

Most of the small combines used the towing tractor's power takeoff, which required that the tractor engine run at constant speed. Constant speed is difficult when the grain crop density varies, or the land is hilly. This machine had its own engine for threshing but we towed it with Dad's Ford tractor or H.B.'s little John Deere. I already drove our Ford tractor at 14, so they enlisted me to help with the harvesting and to learn to operate H.B.'s John Deere.

When they were working in their own fields, Dad and H.B. were fairly relaxed and unhurried. Harvesting with them was fun, particularly when we finished at H.B.'s and he bought a picnic jug of beer to celebrate. Dad didn't drink beer, so I had to uphold the Hoskins end of the jug. After Dad's crop was in, they could work for the neighbors, and that income was pure gravy.

After a couple of years, H.B. bailed out of the combine agreement and sold his share to Dad. I suspect he did so partly because he didn't like to hire out with the machine but mostly because he stopped raising grain and began raising livestock. Dad and I, in order to support the combine, harvested other folks' grain in earnest.

Part of the fun of harvesting for other people was the generous meals we were served. We usually asked that dinner (for you non-farmers, that's the noon meal) be brought to the field to save time (and washing up). Sometimes our meal was served on camp plates, sometimes on everyday dishes. One lady, however, sent good china, good silver and linen napkins with dinner. I was always glad to thresh for her. On the other hand, one family brought dry cheese sandwiches and buttermilk. Since they were Mormon, we didn't expect coffee. Outraged, Dad decided he wasn't hungry, but those folks had a raft of kids, and I wonder if perhaps that wasn't the very best they had.

One of our hardest jobs was combining for a farmer who raised wheat on dry-land sandhills. Some of the dunes were too steep for the tractor to climb pulling the combine. The owner didn't worry about steep hills. What the heck—he farmed with horses. I tried cutting along the slope, but the combine slid sideways, and there was nothing I could do but to turn downhill and "ride her down." I drove around to a gentler slope to the top of the hill, drove empty to the steep slope, and combined downhill. To maintain a reasonable speed that ensured the combine cut cleanly, I braked the tractor going down the hill. This became a bit touchy, because there were a two or three tons of combine with no brakes at all, racing the tractor. A couple of times I thought the combine might win, but I made it in a dead heat.

The shaker rack for that machine was supported by cast fittings with bearings on a tapered bolt which ensured a tight fit. They were the very devil to get off, and of course, the bearings did eventually wear out. More often, the cast fittings broke, from metal fatigue, I suppose. Either failure required that the tapered bolt be removed from the shaker rack itself.

Imagine this picture. Way back inside this little tiny combine is a bolt that must be driven out with a two pound hammer. Get, also, this picture. A heavy-set man in his fifties and a skinny kid in his teens. Guess who draws the short straw and gets to crawl into the guts of the combine and beat that bolt out?

The racks must have been all of eight or nine inches apart, so here lies poor me on my back, bare to the waist (it was HOT in there) on a rack that would make a fakir flinch. I'm swinging a two-pound hammer across my face, beating on a bolt I can barely see. With each stroke of the hammer, another cloud of chaff falls on my eyes, nose, and ears. I can't even cuss—I'd get a mouthful of chaff. Then, from outside:

"Are ya havin' any fun?"

Blue smoke comes rolling out of the combine.

One evening when the humidity was low we worked long after sundown. It was nearly dark when I noticed a cloud hanging over the combine. I thought it must be smoking excessively, so I pointed the cloud out to Dad.

"Holy smoke!" he said.

I saw nothing holy about it.

"That's not smoke. That's SKEETERS!"

119

We hurried to shut down the machine for the night, hoping to be finished before the mosquitoes descended. Shutting down took time. A canvas belt with slats across it carried grain and straw to the combine's maw. If we left the canvas tight during the night, it stretched, and the next day it slipped. So, to shut down, we had to loosen the springs that held the canvas taut. It was a time-consuming process—doubly so with several hundred thousand mosquitoes gnawing at our vitals. When we finally got through, we were weak from loss of blood.

Start-up took quite some time, too, and we'd be in the field at least two hours before the dew was off if we could. When there was no dew, we'd be there at daylight, having done our regular farm chores—milking the cows, feeding the stock, setting the irrigation water, pestering Mother at breakfast. We had to put gas in the combine and the tractor, grease all the bearings—some of which were placed so only a contortionist with pronounced tics could reach them—and tightening those loosened canvases.

For those who have never operated a combine or other threshing machine, I take time here to explain the "cylinder." When the grain (or whatever) first enters the machine, it is thrashed by a rotating set of bars. If it were solid, this would, indeed, be a cylinder. The cylinder turned past a set of stationary bars with just enough clearance to allow the crop being threshed to pass through. Any large wad jammed the cylinder and brought the machine to a halt.

When we threshed clover seed, the combine picked up long windrows of clover hay. The clover was cut and windrowed while it was still green, and lay in the field until it dried. This sometimes took a week or two—especially if we had rain—giving whirlwinds time to form and ravage through the windrows, piling the clover up in places, leaving other places bare. In order to thresh those piles, we pulled the combine up alongside and pitched the hay in carefully, because overloading the cylinder choked the combine down, sometimes to a complete stop. At such times, we were glad the cylinder was not solid. Someone (why was it always me?) had to climb inside and dig the wad out, sometimes straw by straw. I could grab a cylinder bar and rotate the cylinder back and forth a millimeter or so to help loosen things up. All this with the sun burning my back and Dad yelling at me to hurry up.

Straw wads weren't the only worry. An occasional nesting pheasant might be slow to flee the combine and be forced up with the grain. The cylinder must have been vegetarian—it balked at pheasant, although by the time it stopped, the pheasant was in no condition to be kept for meat.

A big bull thistle with a stalk a couple of inches across was a sure show-stopper. Pulling a thistle out required tough hands and considerable verbal assistance. Seems to me some of the words we used were "#$%*&I" and "^$%&*@%$**" and sometimes even "oh, for pity's sake." Dad always teased me about wearing gloves, saying I couldn't get anything done with leather gloves on. I noticed when there was a thistle in the cylinder, it was, "You got gloves. Go pull it out."

One of us sometimes walked just ahead of the machine carrying a pitchfork and toss the thistles out of the windrow to prevent jamming and the use of such language. I told you about one instance in which the language slipped out when I pinned my foot to the ground with the pitchfork.[10]

---

[10]See "Peerless Tobacco and a Pocket Knife." *More Montana: Tall Tales, Damn Lies and Otherwise* page 33.

Each evening, the chaff and dust from the combine left us looking like we'd been rooting in the dirt and feeling like we'd been rolling in itching powder. The worst chaff came when we were threshing oats. The outer hull of the oat threshes up into tiny straws smaller than a hair, and those little devils get right into your pores and require lots of scrubbing to get them out. They are much worse than hair clippings. The nearest I can come to describing oat chaff is to compare it with nettles, and if you've never been into stinging nettles—well, you just can't imagine.

Every now and again, as I drive past a combine working in the fields, I'm tempted to go out and hitch a ride for a round or two. The dust, the chaff, the heat would bring back familiar memories. And remind me of why I left the farm in the first place.

Lost Cause?

Penelope Pope
Has given up hope
Of finding a husband, she says.
The fellow she likes
Has four little tykes
And a wife who is still working days.

Confession

Some years ago, a group of hunters in the Mission Mountains came across an elk skull sporting a magnificent rack of horns. The extraordinary condition made them wonder. The horns were tied to a couple of fir trees with what appeared to be a halter rope. There was some conjecture about the skill of the guy who could tie an elk like that, and also some discussion of what kind of a lousy S.O.B. would tie up the poor animal and leave it to starve.

It's been a long time. Now that I have firmly established my reputation for veracity, I can tell the truth of the story.

The snow had fallen in the high country. I knew the elk were moving down; so the day before elk season opened, I rode into the Missions to scout for a good hunting spot. I tied my horse and climbed a rocky knoll to look around. When I came back, the blankety-blank horse had slipped his halter and wandered away. I never claimed I was too smart about tying up a saddle horse.

I picked up the halter and the few feet of rope on it and set out to find that missing horse. I wasn't being too careful, just following the horse tracks, when I started a big bull elk from his bed. He jumped up and must have gotten out of the wrong side of that bed, because he was more than a bit irritable. He shook his rack and started toward me.

I forgot about chasing horses and made for a stand of white fir hoping, to get up the tree ahead of those horns. I didn't make it. Just before I got to the trees I saw elk horns on both sides of me, and thought I'd bought the farm for sure. The elk pushed me against a tree, but his rack was so wide that a point or two stuck into the tree on each side. I don't know whether the old boy was trying to get free or to take those trees down, but I had a few seconds and without really giving it much thought, I threw a quick dally on the horns on one side, dodged around the tree and tied the other end of the rope to the horns on the other. I had that elk tied solidly to the trees.

I have never hunted for sport. I have said before and I'll say again: I was a meat hunter. And here stood several hundred pounds of prime elk meat. I left the elk trying to knock those trees down and went to catch my horse. He was easy. He hadn't found anything interesting to eat in the snow and knew I had some grain in the feed bag on the saddle, but he couldn't reach that. I got back on him and rode out.

Next day, the first day of the season, I went back for my elk. My horse started acting nervous when we were a couple hundred yards away from where I'd left the elk. I supposed he knew the elk was good and mad, so I kept going. When we rounded the fir stand from the other side, the biggest grizzly I ever hope to see rose up. Now, I hadn't lost any grizzlies, and neither had that saddle horse, and we scorched a trail away from there that not even the grizzly could follow.

I never went back. As far as I was concerned one grizzly was a heap too many and he could have the elk.

So there's the truth to the tied elk. I didn't leave it to starve, didn't intend to, but I didn't get an elk that year. That damn bear did, though.

The Crossing

Owen had been awake much of the night, waiting for light, listening to the heavy rain drumming on their lean-to tent and the rushing wind shaking it as if it were trying to lift the little shelter from them. In the cold dawn, he watched the water rising over the flat bottom land all the way to the river and he worried that they might not be able to get home. The road was completely covered, indiscernible under the flood; the little ridge where they were camped was all that stood above water. Jason stood shivering beside him, looking up for reassurance. Owen hated himself for putting his son in what had turned out to be serious danger, and wished he had not brought Jason along this time.

"Still rising. We'll have to try to make it across on the log," he said, as much to himself as to Jason.

The log was really a tall pine that had blown down the winter before. When Owen hauled the logs from this camp, he drove the team and wagon over the road that wound along the river; but when he came to fell the trees, he usually walked, and the tree had fallen in a convenient place to form a footbridge. Two days ago he had brought Jason to the camp—supposedly to help, but mostly for company. The boy had been proud and happy to think that his father needed his nine-year-old help. That day they had come down from the prairie and laughed as they bounced and balanced on the springy log, six feet above the lazily flowing creek.

Owen picked up the knapsack and a few biscuits for their breakfast along the way.

"Come," he said, and sloshed out into the rain.

The mud made walking difficult. Jason soon lagged behind, and Owen turned and motioned impatiently to him, then felt a pang of conscience. Jason was doing his best to keep up.

Owen breathed a small prayer of thanks when he saw that the tree was still there. The stream that had been little more than a trickle a few days ago now brushed against the lower edge of the log, making it tremble and bow downstream. The brush of branches thrashed against the near bank. It looked as if it could go anytime. He would get Jason across, at least, and then hope for himself.

"Jase," he said, "you go on ahead. Looks like the water's about to take her out. I'm gonna stay here and try to hold her." He stepped in water to his waist, braced against the mass of branches and nodded to Jason.

Jason looked at him and started to speak, but then obediently stepped up on the log. When his muddy boot slipped and he almost lost his balance, Owen's heart dropped. Oh, God. Let him be strong. Jason recovered and started across the shaking, twisting log.

Owen struggled to hold the tree against the tug of the current, and found himself holding his breath as he watched Jason stepping carefully along but growing more confident as the tree trunk widened nearer its base.

A sudden gush of water shook the log, and Jason lost his balance and began to fall. Owen cried out and made ready to dive in after him but Jason managed to catch the log, his legs in the swirl downstream. He looked back once, then climbed slowly back onto the log and, crept along, finally scrambling rapidly the last few feet until he could catch one of the roots. Owen breathed again.

The tree was really shaking now, and in the center, the water flowed over the log. When Owen loosed the branches, it seemed the tree moved. He climbed hurriedly

126

up and stepped onto the log to steady it, then ran toward his son.

He was halfway across when the bouncing log began to swing downstream, pivoting on its base, still anchored by a few unbroken roots. Owen danced and twisted to keep his footing and to maintain his balance, and ran the last few steps leaning over the water. He would have fallen in had he not been able to catch a root and balance himself. He swept Jason up with one arm, jumped from the tree base to the bank, and struggled up the muddy slope to the safety of the hill above.

At the top of the bank, he reluctantly put the boy down, and they turned to look back at the flood below. Their bridge now swung in the current, tenuously held by a few roots that soon would give way. Owen clapped his son on the shoulder—too hard; it made Jason wince.

"You sure looked funny crawling up the last few feet there," he said.

"Well, you did a pretty good dance yourself," Jason said crossly. He looked up, and Owen grinned down at him. Jason began to grin too, and soon they were both laughing hysterically as they started across the prairie to the farm. Owen knew his wife was worried sick, and she'd scold both of them for tracking in the mud, but he also knew that the show of anger would be relief. He knew, too, that Jason was already embellishing the story he would tell to his sisters about how they'd beaten the raging creek.

The Log

Jason woke to the sounds of the storm. The heavy rain drummed on the tent and the rushing wind made it flap as if it wished to fly away from them. Jason shivered when he saw water all around the little ridge where they were camped. The road on which his father drove the team and wagon when he hauled logs from this camp was gone, hidden under a newborn lake.

Two days ago Jason had come to the camp with his father, and he had been proud and happy that his father needed his nine-year-old help. Jason shivered and looked to his father for reassurance. His father studied the water a few moments before he spoke.

"Still rising. We'll have to try to make it across on the log."

Near the walking path a big tree had fallen to bridge the gully where the little creek flowed. Jason liked to leave the path and walk across on the log. In the middle, he jumped up and down to make the log spring and threaten to throw him into the creek below.

His father abruptly picked up the knapsack, said "Come," and sloshed out into the rain.

Jason followed and found the rain cool but not uncomfortable. His clothing was already damp; it had not dried completely from the soaking he'd gotten yesterday helping saw the trees. He tried to keep up with his father's long stride, but he could hardly walk in slithery mud. His father turned and motioned angrily to him, and he rushed as fast as he could to catch up.

Jason would not have recognized the tree but for the familiar root mass across on the far side of the creek. The stream that he could have stepped across a few days ago was now a torrent flowing against the full length of the

128

log. The log trembled as if trying to decide to let go and float downstream. Jason looked up at his father.

"Jase," his father said, "you go on ahead. Looks like the water's about to take her out. I'm gonna stay here and try to hold her." He waded in up to his waist, seized the branches and nodded to Jason.

Jason knew what he had to do, but his sanity rebelled against walking out onto the shaking log. Obediently, he stepped up but his muddy boot slipped and he almost fell. He looked down at his father, and saw anger in the man's face. Why's he mad at me, Jason wondered. Best to go. He knew better than to disobey, especially when his father was already angry.

The log shook and twisted as the stream tried to claim it. Jason tried to ignore the flowing water, knowing it could mesmerize him if he watched it. He stepped carefully along, but grew bolder as the tree trunk widened nearer its base. Suddenly the log shook under the assault of the water. Jason lost his balance, fell, and slid off the log. He managed to catch and hold a limb, his legs in the swirling stream. He looked back at his father straining against the tree, and knew he had to do this on his own. He climbed back onto the log and crept on hands and knees until he reached one of the roots. He turned to watch his father scramble up and stand on the precarious bridge. The tree shook, and the water flowing over the log made Jason fear the tree was going to break free. His father started slowly, then ran toward him. When he was halfway across, the bouncing log began to move, and the tree began to swing downstream, a few unbroken roots holding it from floating clear away. Jason watched his father twist and dance to maintain his balance, but fear kept him fixed to the root in his hand. He closed his eyes, unwilling to watch his father die. Suddenly a strong arm swept him up and his father was carrying him up the muddy slope to the safety of the hill above.

At the top of the bank, his father put him down, and they turned to look back at the flood below. The log now swung downstream, barely held by a few roots. His father clapped him on the shoulder, hard enough to hurt.

"You sure looked funny crawling up the last few feet there," he said.

"Well, you did a pretty good dance yourself," Jason said crossly. He looked up, and his father was grinning. Jason couldn't help it; he began to grin too, and soon they were both laughing as they started across the prairie to the farm. Mom would have dry clothes, and he was already forming an exaggerated story to tell his sisters about his heroism and how they'd beaten the swollen creek.

Counterstroke

I didn't want the work in the first place. The owner of the place, a friend of mine, had contracted out the job but the contractor couldn't seem to get enough help. I told my friend I'd work a week just to get him out of a hole.

I had some little experience with heavy equipment; so since the back hoe operator hadn't shown up, the contractor boss put me on the back hoe. After a few false starts, I got the controls partially memorized and set to work digging a trench. Nothing I did was right, according to the boss. Either the trench wasn't straight or it wasn't wide enough or I was too slow. He accompanied each complaint with a profane and disparaging description of me and my ancestry. It only took a few such remarks to get under my skin, but he was a burly two hundred fifty pounds and I didn't dare confront him. I stuck it out, seething all the time, planning some kind of retaliation. Friday, at the end of the promised week, I still hadn't thought of a suitable punishment.

The trench I was digging ran so close to the portable toilet that I worried I might hit the structure, but the boss refused to move it. It had been there all week, and he'd wait until the biffy owner's crew came and have them move it, rather than using his employees' valuable time. I was digging right behind the biffy when the boss entered it. Seldom has Providence given me such an opportunity. I eased the hoe over to the biffy, then with one quick stroke tipped the thing over onto the door side. The week-old contents of the tank poured out through cracks around the door, and, from the sound of his curses, all over the boss.

I don't know how long it took for someone to right the biffy and free the boss, because I was long gone down the road, happy as can be, without a care in the world.

The Loons

When we weren't crashing elevators into the ground,[11] Bill and I fished for food. We spent more on gas than the value of the fish we caught. We were skunked so many times, I considered reviving my nickname, "Stinker." Nevertheless, when the 1950 season opened in mid-April, we planned to be on the water on Williams Lake at dawn. We drove to the lake and parked, planning to sleep in the car. We were settling into our blankets when the resort manager came to our car window and knocked.

"You fellas planning to sleep here tonight?"

"Well, yes. We didn't think anyone would object."

"It's gonna be damn cold tonight. Nobody's in the cabins. Why don't you sleep in one of them? Long as you don't mess it up."

I could almost have kissed him. I was already cold and cramped in the car. We moved our blankets into the cabin, built a fire to take the chill off, bragged a bit on the fish we'd catch the next day and turned in. Next morning I woke first. Well, I got up first. I'm not sure Bill wasn't playing possum. I made coffee and waved a cup under his nose, waking him thoroughly. We were glad we'd slept inside. During the night a heavy frost had covered everything, including the car windows and the boats.

We dragged a boat to the water, scraped some of the frost off the seats and rowed out as the sun rose. Nobody else was on the lake, and the only sound was the splash of our oars and the chatter of our teeth. We selected a spot by guesswork, dropped anchor and set about fishing. In an

---

[11]See "The Down Side," *Building Character:Tales from Montana (And Other Damn Lies)* page 145.

hour or so, the sun began to take some of the chill off, and our spirits rose.

We sat and fished. We fished and sat. Our hands were so cold we could barely bait a hook; but that wasn't necessary anyhow, because no fish touched our bait. We tried different depths and different bait. No action. We moved to another location and had no luck. Back at our original spot, two guys in another boat hooked fish after fish. We said, in unison, "For pity's sake." A snow squall blew across the lake, the temperature dropped even lower, but we had come to *fish*, and no little old squall was going to stop us. We hunkered down to freeze and fish.

After lunch, I felt I needed a smoke. In those days I couldn't afford cigarettes, so I smoked a cheap pipe with cheap tobacco. I filled my pipe, took out my trusty Zippo lighter with a flame like a blowtorch, and took my first puff just as my rod went over the side. I grabbed the rod a full arm-length into the water, and began to play the fish. I had it almost to the boat when my line went slack. What I said then cannot be reported here.

I re-baited my hook, and let the line out again before I looked for my pipe. There it was on the bottom of the boat, with the tobacco still in it. My tobacco pouch was in the other end of the boat by Bill. The Zippo? I found it under the seat, still blazing merrily away.

That was the sum total of our strikes that day.

As I huddled miserably there in the boat, my soaked arm slowly turning to ice, a loon called from the end of the lake. It sounded like, "Haw, Haw, Haw, Haw."

"Up your ass," I muttered.

Bill laughed until he nearly fell from the boat. Then he pulled up the anchor, grabbed the oars and began rowing us back to the dock.

Skunked again.

133

Bear Repellent

When we arrived at the cabin, one bear sat on his haunches across the stream and four more hung around up the hill toward the ridge. Apparently some of the summer visitors hadn't understood the "don't feed the bears" policy, and these guys were still looking for a handout. Glenda wanted to cancel the weekend right then, but Tom and I convinced her that Snuffy, a clumsy part-English Sheepdog, would drive the bears off. We lied. Snuffy wouldn't have frightened a housecat, let alone a bear. Tom and I knew that, if the bears found no food, they would soon drift away.

Tom and Glenda had rented the cabin off season, so of the several in the camp, only ours was occupied. The sturdily built cabins were perhaps not bear-proof, but were certainly bear-resistant.

While we unloaded the car, I kept an eye on the bears, trying to determine whether they really were a threat. The sight of Glenda storing canned food in the low shelves distracted me. She was wearing short shorts, and the view, as she bent over, was captivating. Apparently Snuffy was a dirty old man too, because he walked over and poked his nose on her rear.

I heard the first part of her scream, before it rose to a pitch higher than I could hear. Snuffy put his head down and his paws over his ears. The bear on the other side of the stream took off like a shot, and the other bears trotted over the ridge, stopping now and then to rub their heads, as if their ears hurt.

Snuffy avoided Glenda for the rest of the trip, and we saw no more evidence of bears.

I wish I could package that scream. Best bear repellent a person could ask for.

A Moving Experience

In June of 1958, Western Electric Company transferred me from Spokane, Washington, to New Jersey. We had six children at the time, and were expecting the seventh in September. Western Electric did not transfer employees with large families capriciously. Living expenses eat into profits, so I'm sure the decision to move us was well thought out. And possibly regretted, later.

We owned one of the first Volkswagen Microbuses in the country. It held our family, but its 37-horsepower engine had a hard time hauling us over the mountains. I'm sure we were cursed a number of times when drivers of larger cars wanted to pass. I know I avoid VW buses even now, even though their engines are much more powerful. One advantage of the bus, though, was the camaraderie we enjoyed with other Microbus owners. They were so few that we waved and honked at each other like long lost relatives.

In New Jersey, Western put us up at a motel, in two rooms with single-room air conditioners that worked part time. The younger children spent much of their time watching television, which, in 1958, was not nearly so sophisticated as it is today. One station played its "Movie of the Week" every day for a week. The kids watched *No Time for Sergeants* so many times they memorized the dialogue and could even do a passable job on Andy Griffith's accent.

The older boys, who were nine, eight, seven and six years old, explored around the motel for entertainment. Since the place was quite new, most of the immediate environs consisted of bare earth, muddy hills, and a small stream amidst the poison ivy. Cabin fever was rampant, but we were stuck. To buy a house in New Jersey, we needed to sell our house in Spokane, but the departure of an air wing from Spokane had depressed the economy there and houses weren't selling. Western Electric offered to buy the house, but red tape and paperwork proliferated and The O'Reilly and the kids whiled away the time in the motel, bouncing from wall to wall. (Imagine a seven-months- pregnant woman doing *that*.)

After a few weeks of motel living—during which time the company was paying our expenses, including meals for eight people—I suggested to the powers that existed that perhaps we could find a summer rental for less money where we could at least do our own cooking. This, I suggested, might be better for all concerned, since we'd have more freedom and the expenses would decrease by something like half. The idea sold, after some initial red-tape cutting, and we moved to a summer cabin on Lake Hopatcong. Lake Hopatcong was, and maybe still is, a major summer retreat.

We rented a cabin named "Fool's Folly." It was about as much retreat as one could find. It was, in fact, more nearly a rout. The cabin had been built one room at a time, the additions tacked on helter-skelter. The shower, a galvanized tin stall just off the kitchen, had no close connection to the rest of the bathroom facilities. The dark, dank living room was two steps down from the rest of the house and, until we got used to it, provided practice in falling for all members of the family. One morning on the way to work, I stepped from the upper level to the living room floor without using the steps in between, and stepped right through the rotten living room floor. By the time I got my foot extricated, I was late for work.

After a couple of weeks, the owners wanted to use their cabin, so we were forced to look elsewhere. A few doors away we found a nearly new cabin with a loft in which we could bunk the four older boys comfortably. And the rent was nearly the same.

One evening we had bacon and eggs for supper. Kevin, then six, went to the kitchen for something and spilled the can of hot bacon grease down his front. He was wearing shorts, and so had a broad burn from collar bone to the shorts line. He was fortunate the shorts were there. He looked at the burn, saw how upset we were, and asked, "Will I die, Daddy?" Not if I could help it. I took him and his eight-year-old brother Jim (for solace and company) and set out looking for a hospital. Kevin was in little pain—at least he didn't complain. We came to a sheriff's substation, and asked directions. When I told them the problem, the deputies insisted we get in their patrol car, and they drove us to the hospital with red lights running, but without the siren. (The kids would have liked the siren.) Jim and I settled Kevin in the hospital bed and rode back with the deputies, *sans* red lights, this time.

Next day, The O'Reilly and I somehow found a baby sitter (or maybe left the kids with the eight- and nine-year-olds) and went to the hospital to visit Kevin. As we got out of the car, the nurses came running with a wheelchair, and tried to seat The O'Reilly in it. She was, by this time, eight months pregnant, and looked ready to deliver. The delivery room nurses were disappointed, but they said, cheerfully, "Well, we'll see you soon." (They didn't. The baby was born at a different hospital.)

Red tape still held up the sale of our house. One day the whole family descended[12] on Company headquarters in New York to sign another of the interminable series of forms. We took headquarters by storm. A mid-level

---

[12]Probably I should say "ascended" since we went to the 74th floor.

manager left his desk and escorted us around, showing off this "wonderful family." I suspect that he, too, was Catholic and appreciated big families. We sat around for a few minutes waiting for someone to come up with the paperwork, and created a stir, to put it mildly. When the formalities were finished, we were assured that the rest of the paperwork would be processed promptly. It was. I think the bosses were afraid we'd invade again.

We bought a house and moved into it the first of September. We had heard how cold and unfriendly the New Jersey folks were, so we expected to be isolated and alone. But no matter where you are, if your kids are the age of your neighbors', you'll make friends. (Or enemies.) The neighbor women welcomed The O'Reilly with more than open arms.

Theresa Ann Hoskins was born less than three weeks after we moved into the house. After taking The O'Reilly to the hospital, I settled down to take care of the kids— until one of the neighbors showed up.

"What are you doing here? Why aren't you at the hospital? Your wife needs you."

I explained that someone had to look after the kids.

"I'll take care of them. You get out of here."

So, I went to the hospital and waited until our pretty little girl was born. When I came home, the neighbor was doing our ironing. This was the neighbor who had confided to The O'Reilly that, of all household chores, she hated ironing the most. Cold New Jersey neighbors? Tell me about it.

The O'Reilly had balked at camping, the only entertainment our large family could afford. But when she recalled how primitive our early life in New Jersey had been, she agreed to try the outdoor life. She liked it, and we have enjoyed camping in half the lower forty states.

Practical Joker

I want to explain here that I do not believe in practical jokes that cause pain, expense, or public humiliation. I do, however, like the mild, more subtle kind.

Once in a while, it is my great pleasure to come across a person who's just right to lie to, someone who will swallow anything (even the stories in this book)—and the bigger the whopper, the more he or she will believe it. Once in a while I come across a fellow who is a perfect target for a practical joke. Such a person is rare. He (less often, she) must be a bit pompous but still have a well-developed sense of humor. Bob was one of those persons. He was a bit stuffy, and believed strongly in proprieties.

We were working at Bell Telephone Laboratories at the time of these events. Bob and I were two of the five men in an office long enough for three desks to fit end-to-end along each wall, with space for file cabinets at the end near the door. The office was just wide enough so that the chairs of the two persons on opposite sides of the room seldom collided. Protocol (at least, that's what Bob said) dictated that the senior Bell Telephone engineer have the desk next to the window with the light over his *left* shoulder. The next senior engineer had the desk behind him, with light from the window over his *right* shoulder.

When I moved into the office, I was a Western Electric engineer, and didn't rate a window seat. Bob was senior with the light over his left shoulder, and a senior technician (not engineer) had the other window seat. It will give you an insight into Bob's personality to know that when I transferred from Western Electric to Bell Labs (this was before the AT&T breakup) he made a fuss and wanted me to eject the technician and take the window seat. I'm not sure he ever forgave me for my breach of propriety when I refused.

The Navy owned the building in which we worked, and, to facilitate restructuring the offices, the walls were bolted to the floor and could be unbolted and moved, sometimes overnight. So that they were sturdy enough to withstand frequent moving, they were made of steel layers with two or three inches of sound insulation between the sheets. The steel walls were essential to our ultimate practical joke.

Practical jokes were common at Bell Labs. A frequently used material was the punchings from IBM cards, called chad. Alas, office workers of today, sitting at their PCs, don't even know what an IBM card is, much less chad. Chad was fine, dusty stuff which clung tenaciously to suit material, and many a stuffy engineer found his desk drawer booby-trapped with an arrangement that flung chad in his face.

Another common joke involved a paper clip bent into a "U" shape with a rubber band across the legs. A small piece of IBM card (there's that mysterious dinosaur again) wound in the rubber band made a startling sound when released from a tightly packed file folder.

In our office, we were more sophisticated. Once we arranged a small box filled with punches from a three-hole punch in the light fixture above Bob's chair, with a fine wire connected to the back of his central desk drawer. When he opened his desk, it snowed. Flakes held up for a while by static electricity fell intermittently all day. And Bob swore softly but laughingly with each flake.

The building was not air conditioned, and we opened the windows to let in what little air New Jersey offered. The screens failed to keep out the common houseflies, a nuisance most of us could not stand. We had no swatters;

we used rubber bands. If one sneaks up on a fly within the length of his rubber band, he can obliterate the fly. This required more time and stealth than we wished to expend, so we simply shot the rubber bands at the flies. We knocked them off the wall regularly, and we got so good we could sometimes pick a fly off in midair. Bob did not indulge. One day, he made the mistake of remarking that if we were to kill these flies, we should at least give them a decent burial.

Bob was involved in a project which required him to travel frequently. His travels allowed us time for more elaborate jokes. Next time he returned from a trip, the floor behind and around his chair was a fly graveyard, with each fly carcass sporting a cardboard (guess where we got the cardboard) headstone. Some headstones bore crosses, some Stars of David, one or two had a crescent, and others simply said "Rest in Peace." The assignments were guesswork—we didn't ask the fly his religion before we downed him. Bob wondered why the janitors hadn't swept the graveyard away, so we told him that he was doing so much highly secret work the janitors believed us when we warned them not to disturb Bob's experiment.

We set up our greatest and final joke while Bob was again away on a trip. I suppose office workers in the present cubicles pin things to the walls. At Bell Labs, the most common decorations were meeting schedules, inter-office memos of little import, and other reminders. Since the walls were steel, we couldn't use thumbtacks, so we used small magnets of the type that were used on very small loudspeakers. At the time we pulled this prank, magnets had been hard to get.

While Bob was away on a trip, we demagnetized three magnets, and replaced three from Bob's wall. One of the displaced magnets held some rings of the type used to hold punched paper together loosely. A second held up a cartoon, and the third held a sheaf of memoranda. Using rubber cement, we carefully glued two magnets to the wall, and managed to hang the rings and the cartoon so they looked undisturbed. The sheaf of memoranda we laid on the desk with a magnet on it. I hid his three good magnets in my desk drawer.

I wasn't in the office when Bob returned to his desk, but I met him in the hall shortly afterward. I greeted him and he responded with a curt hello and some mumbling about magnets. I sped back to our office as quickly as Bell Labs decorum allowed, and found one of the plotters there. He gave this account.

Bob came in, obviously tired and out of sorts, saw the stack of papers on his desk with a magnet on them, put the papers on the wall with the magnet and let go. The whole thing fell to the desk. He tried again, but this time he held the papers after he let the magnet go. The magnet fell. He tried it again. It fell. He took the magnet holding the cartoon (which fell to the desk) and used it, letting go of magnet and papers. All fell to the desk. He gathered up the papers, pulled off the magnet holding the rings and tried it. It wouldn't hold either. He tried the magnet, which had held the rings with some force, on various parts of the wall. It refused to stick anywhere. Disgusted, Bob stormed out of the office.

"Where'd he put the magnets?" I asked.

"He threw them in the wastebasket."

I retrieved the bad magnets, replacing them with the good ones—just in time. Here came Bob.

"What was it you said to me in the hall? Something about magnets?" I was all innocence.

"You guys ruined my magnets while I was gone," Bob growled.

"Ruined your magnets? What do you mean? Magnets are hard to come by. Nobody'd ruin magnets."

"Well, they don't work."

"Where are these ruined magnets?"

"There. In the trash."

I searched through the wastebasket and found the magnets. I tried them on my wall, and of course they stuck.

"Well, if you don't want them, I'll take them," I said.

"Gimme those." Bob grabbed the magnets and tried them on his wall. They worked fine. He replaced the items as they had been, and sat down at his desk with his head in his hands. We "innocents" went quietly to work.

We could almost hear him thinking, "How can this happen? I have a Masters degree in Physics and another in Electrical Engineering. Surely I can figure this out." After some time, he raised his head and addressed us all.

"I don't know how you did it, but you sure got to me this time," he said, smiling for the first time that day. Then we all laughed.

But we never told him how we did it. That was our last, our ultimate practical joke on Bob. Anything more would have been too dull.

The THING

Once in a while, in my career as an engineer, my management called upon me to present a paper on the findings of a study or on some facet of my group's work. I think the main reason was my familiarity with the English language and the fact that I'm one of those rare engineers who can write an intelligible sentence. On one occasion, I was scheduled for an early morning (nine o'clock is very early when you've been partying all night) presentation. As the group of us from North American Aviation wandered over to the lecture hall, if I may call it that, we passed a display of assorted pieces of the Apollo space module. Since our company made the spacecraft, many of the pieces in the display were familiar to one or more of our group. One, though, was a puzzle to us all. It resembled a metal helmet cast of aluminum, with several small chains welded to the dome, each attached to a one-inch pin. We picked it up and examined it but no one could think of the faintest notion of what it could be. When it came my turn to examine it, I looked it over, and found a hole bored into one edge. The hole seemed to have no purpose, and I wondered if perhaps it was threaded inside. I felt around with my finger, and, sure enough there were threads in there. So was my finger. It was caught and would not come out. I asked my companions for help, and amid much laughter, we tried everything but amputation. The finger held.

As we worked, we were aware that nine o'clock was fast approaching, but nothing helped. Then the call came for us to get up to the presentation, and I realized I was "on" in five minutes. What to do with the THING? We redoubled our efforts, but the only result was a badly sprained finger that threatened to swell and make matters worse. My supervisor, unaware of the problem, pushed me forward when the moderator announced my name. With my notes in my right hand, the THING on my left, I approached the dais. I was tempted to explain my predicament, but the snickers of my peers and the burning glare of my supervisor made that seem like a bad idea. So I made my presentation. As I remember, it had to do with our simulation of the space flight in orbit, and the mathematical manipulations we used to describe the rotations of a free floating body. It really was quite complex.

The THING lay in the lectern quietly until I turned a page of my notes, at which it moved slightly and the chains tinkled against the body. The microphone picked up the noise and the sound system amplified it and carried it throughout the hall, louder than my voice. A dozing engineer in the back row abruptly sat up and looked interested, and I realized that suddenly my audience was listening, rapt, to what I had to say. But I also noticed that all eyes were not on me, but were on the THING, especially each time it announced its presence with the rattle of chains. Seldom has a technical paper been so closely attended. When I finished with the paper, I was about to ask for questions, as was the custom. Instead, I decided to bite the bullet and explain the THING.

"I know some of you, many of you, are interested in what this"—I raised the THING above the lectern—"is and what it has to do with our mathematical model. The answers are, I don't know and nothing. You see, just before I came up here, we were looking at this THING and wondering what it was and I got my finger stuck in it and can't get it out."

I have never, before or since, received such an ovation. The crowd stood and laughed and hooted and clapped and whistled. I'm sure many remembered their own mishaps resulting from curiosity. The only one not laughing was my boss, and he sat there looking like he wanted to strangle me.

At the reception that evening, several engineers from other companies hunted me up to discuss our mutual problem.

"I seldom pay much attention to tech papers," a Grumman engineer told me, "but you truly captured us. I'll remember all you said forever. That's the greatest gimmick I ever saw. What made you think of that, anyway?"

"Oh, it was just a sudden inspiration," I said, waving the THING in his face.

Liberated Woman?

Young Julia Plink
Has taken to drink—
Not liquor, but sour buttermilk.
She eats what she likes
And rides on her bikes
Wearing only her bloomers of silk.

Bear Burglar

Some folks are too particular about germs. To listen to the current warnings, we should all be like Howard Hughes, so fearful we might catch a bug of some sort we'd isolate ourselves. I grew up on a farm during the not-so-Great Depression, and learned early that one must strike a balance between sanitation and practicality. Our kitchen floor (linoleum) was seldom free from tracked-in mud or manure, but if a morsel of food fell on the floor, I forgot sanitation in my haste to beat the dog to it.

Modern mothers who have pets know that letting the dog lick the baby's face seldom causes harm, and I think that kids who are allowed to get dirty and are allowed to come in contact with germs are often much healthier in the long run than those who are kept too clean and protected. Still, there are those who are really squeamish about little things. Like Glenda. When the bear got into our camp food, she really lost it.

I had gone with Glenda and her husband Tom in their van to camp and hike in the Sierras. We arrived in mid-afternoon, and managed a short hike among the boulders near the camp. At sundown, we returned to camp and ate a camper's dinner of Dinty Moore stew, unbuttered white bread and canned peaches. We sat late around the fire, and watched the moon rise before we closed up the camp.

Heeding the signs warning of bears nearby, we carefully put all the food in the car, checking the windows to make sure there were no slight cracks a bear might get his/her claws into. We made sure to leave no garbage near the camp, and made doubly sure not a crumb of food got into the tents. Satisfied that we were safe from a bear invasion, we retired for a peaceful night. And it was peaceful. Until morning.

I got up early, intending to get everyone started with a good breakfast. When I went to the van, I saw the smaller of our two ice chests wedged between the steering wheel and the dash.

Now, how did that get there? I wondered. I walked around the car to the driver's side and was immediately wide awake. The window on the driver's side was missing, but I saw no broken glass. I looked closely, and could see that the window was down. And that little ice chest had tooth marks in it. We had neglected that one window, and a bear had crawled in and slithered into the back seat. Much of the food was gone from the ice chests. Apparently the bear had eaten all he could get at easily and then tried to take the small chest out to finish it off. When it stuck, he gave it up as a bad job and went on to another smorgasbord.

We were surveying the damage when the people in the RV at the next campsite came out.

"You had a bear last night."

"We know. How did you know?"

"We watched him. He ripped the ice chest open and picked up the salad dressing mixer. He scooted out of the car and loped up the hill. There he sat, licking the salad dressing out. Pretty soon, he came back and got something else. He'd go up the hill, eat it, then come back for more."

"Why didn't you tell us?"

"We didn't want to get involved with a bear. Besides, he was so-o-o-o cute."

In disgust, we finished our inventory.

"How about this carton of milk? It isn't open."

"Throw it away," Glenda said. "I don't want anything with bear spit on it."

"But..."

"Throw it away."

Much of the food was untouched, but we wound up with nothing just because Glenda worried about bear spit. Hell, I'd seen times I'd have gone cheek to jowl with a bear fighting him for the food. As a matter of fact, one of those times happened when we wound up with nothing to eat for breakfast.

Our hiking trip was ended then. We had no food, and we certainly didn't want to camp next to people who thought marauding bears were so cute. Ought to be an open season on such people.

We had breakfast at Burger King at the foot of the mountains.

Earthquake

An earthquake is no laughing matter at the time. If you were on the fringe where the effects were minimal, some of the images of the actual quake are funny enough to be indelibly printed on your memory.

The quake that was to be called the Whittier Earthquake happened between seven and eight in the morning while I was getting ready for work. Our apartment was divided so that the bathroom with the shower was downstairs near the kitchen, and our bedroom was upstairs. My modus operandi was to shower and shave downstairs, then go upstairs to dress. Since only The O'Reilly and I lived there, if I forgot to bring down clean underwear I made the trip upstairs in my bare nakeds. Such was the case on the day of the quake. I had just finished toweling off, and I realized that, once again, my clean shorts were upstairs. I started toward the stairs when I heard the ominous rattle that I knew, from many previous occasions in Southern California, presaged an earthquake. I tried for the kitchen door just before the world began to rock. The refrigerator began to move across the floor, and with typical earthquake mentality (i.e., insanity) I sought to stop its progress. So there I was, waltzing the refrigerator to the tune of the earthquake. Fortunately for me, we were so far from the epicenter that we had no damage. I waltzed the reefer back into place and went ahead getting ready for work.

The day of the major quake in the Bay Area, our son Jim was at a job fair in Silicon Valley. Glassed-in cubicles had been set up on the mezzanine floor of a convention center building.

Jim had finished for the day and was about to leave. His first inkling that he wasn't just dizzy was the crash of glass from those cubicles. He rushed (involuntarily) to the rail overlooking the main floor. He saw the crowd running pell-mell for the exits, and remembers thinking to himself, "I may be killed here, but I'm damned if I'm going to die running and screaming like that." Dignified, I'd call that.

One sight remains in his mind. A slim young woman had lost one of her high-heeled pumps, and was running hippety-hop toward the door on one stocking foot and one high heel. Behind her came a man carrying her other shoe, extending it toward her. In this running screaming melee, all he can think of is returning the lady's shoe. If *that* doesn't prove that chivalry isn't dead, even in an earthquake, I'll eat both shoes.

You might think that you live in an area safe from earthquakes. Well, New York City had one within the last few years. Here in North Idaho we have frequent little tremors, and southern Idaho is ripe for a big one. Even in the center of the country, along the Mississippi River, a really major quake can be expected some day. So get ready to grin and bear it, wherever you are.

Inflight Emergency

Up to that day, I had protected my professional liar status, and hadn't done any charitable lying. Events proved I should have stuck to my principles.

The flight from Heathrow to Los Angeles was, to say the least, boring. That is, until I broke the ice with the handsome woman sitting next to me. Her name, she said, was Margaret, but she was called Peggy. We exchanged information about our careers: I told her I was a professional liar and she confided that she was a registered nurse, working in an emergency room in a suburb of Los Angeles. I even found out she knew my daughter-in-law. We each tried to draw the other out. Talking to someone who did for real what the television shows purportedly enacted intrigued me. She asked the usual questions: what defines a Professional Liar, how does one become one, and so on.

"How do I know you're not lying to me right now?"

"I told you—I'm a professional. I only lie for money."

"Only for money?"

"Well, I guess any professional has to practice. I practice my lies to hone them before I put them in books. And then professionals sometimes teach. But I don't do charity. I suppose you sometimes do some charity work?"

"Of course. I guess most medical professionals do."

"Not me. I lie for money."

"Oh, surely you lie at other times, don't you? I'll bet there are times when you lie out of the goodness of your heart." She was teasing me now.

"I suppose if you count the times I support the story a friend tells his wife about why he's late. Or the times I back up a fishing buddy's estimate of the one that got away. But, hell, any man does that. It has nothing to do with professionalism."

We were nearly halfway through our flight when the aircraft captain, in a stiff-upper-lip British accent, requested that any doctor aboard go to the food service area on the main deck. When he made the announcement for the third time, Peggy rose and went forward toward the announced area.

"Maybe I can help," she said as she left. "There aren't many medical emergencies I haven't seen."

A few minutes later she returned, her face scarlet and her eyes flashing.

"That stinking pig!" She said.

Stinking pig is not exactly the epithet she used, but I don't want to tarnish her image.

"What happened?" I asked.

"There's a guy up there that's about to die. He's got a urinary blockage and he's had it for two days, but he won't let me help him because he's some screwy sect that won't allow a woman's hands do certain things."

"Isn't there any doctor aboard?"

"Yeah, sure. Some pretty, high-heeled, high-priced psychologist. She hasn't run a catheter in fifteen years, and she's afraid to try. Hell, there's nothing to it. I do them every day, sometimes four or five a day. Guess she's afraid to get her pretty little hands dirty. Not that she could. The guy won't let her touch him, either."

"Did you tell the guy you know how?"

"Sure. Well, I think I did. He no spicka da English, and his brother who's interpreting for him isn't much better."

"If he's had this for two days, why's he on this airplane? If it was me, I'd be in the hospital in England."

"How would I know? Well, I gather he was hospitalized a day or two ago. Passed a kidney stone, and thought he was all right. This is what his brother says, I think. Can't be sure, what with the accent and the translation of medical information."

She sat back fuming, and was silent for a while.

"Say!"

She said it so loud I jumped against my seat belt.

"You say you're a true Professional Liar. If you're good at it, you must use some acting talent. Don't you?"

"I never thought of it that way, but I guess I do. The trick is to make a lie sound plausible until you reach the breaking point. Even then, some folks don't catch on."

"What we need is a male doctor. You could look distinguished enough. I'll coach you, and you can take care of the poor guy."

"No way. I ain't gonna shove a tube up some guy's p-p-p-penis."

"Listen. The guy's in agony. Where's your Christian spirit?"

"I don't go for spirits unless they're in a bottle. Tell you what, though. Suppose the guy thinks I'm doing the job and you really are?" The possibilities fascinated me. What a great lie!

"How could we do that? His brother could see."

I already had a scenario in my mind.

"Suppose I'm a doctor that insists there be a curtain so the patient can't see what's going on. We could drape it across his middle and have the stews—ah, flight attendants—hold it so the guy and his brother can't see and I pretend I'm doing the work while you really do. Could we pull that off?"

She smiled for the first time since she came back to her seat.

"You're on," she said, "let's do it. But first, I'm gonna coach you on some medical terms so you'll sound genuine."

154

In the next few minutes she taught me a whole lot more than I ever wanted to know about the male urinary system and how to run a catheter into it.

When we arrived at the food service area this time, the captain was there. He was fuming about having make an emergency detour. He wasn't particularly worried about the patient. He was afraid he'd have to dump fuel and that would be costly for the airline. You'd have thought he owned the damn airplane. Well, maybe he did, pilot's unions being what they are today. Peg introduced me as "Dr. Hoskins" and explained that I'd been asleep at the first call. Pretty darn good liar, that girl. I was accepted without question.

I assumed what I thought would pass for a bedside manner and examined the patient. He lay on the floor with his head on the lap of a man so fat he blocked the aisle. The translator brother, I supposed. "My" patient looked rich. His suit was obviously not from Robert Hall, and he wore a large diamond ring on one hand and a huge ruby on the other. But he was sweaty and his normally dark face was paled to the color of buckskin. His belly looked like he was five months pregnant. I poked it—I knew a real doctor would do that—and found it hard as a melon. The poor guy swore at me through gritted teeth. I didn't understand the words, but the tune of cuss words is the same in any language.

"This man's bladder will burst if we don't catheterize him immediately," I said, remembering Peg's coaching. "What medical equipment do we have?"

The on-board emergency kit contained a catheter and two pairs of rubber gloves, among other things. Peg pulled me aside for a whispered conference.

"They don't have a lubricant."

"A what?" I had a sudden image of giving this guy a grease job and oil change.

"A lubricant. KY or something like that."

"Do you have to have it?"

"Would you like me to do this to *you* dry?"

I shuddered as I imagined that.

"Listen. Do you have your shaving kit along? With some shave cream?"

"Yeah, sure."

"Go get it." I always thought the doctor gave the orders.

When I came back with the shaving cream, one of the stew—flight attendants was pouring out bottles of Perrier.

"Got have something to catch this in," Peggy whispered.

I assumed my "doctor's" role and began to order preparations. Peggy held the rubber gloves and I jammed my hands into them as she'd told me. She put on the other pair and we got down to business. I had two flight attendants hold a blanket so the patient and his brother couldn't see what was actually going on, and a third stand by with the empty Perrier bottles. As Peggy inserted the tube, I tried not to cringe, and kept up a mumbled commentary, remembering to mention some of the precautions she had told me one must take. In no time at all, she was through.

That catheter became a miniature fire hose. The pressure was so great that the tube whipped around, spraying in every direction before we got it secured in a bottle. Changing bottles was a challenge, too, and we spilled a bit each time, on us, on the patient, on the deck. The odor, in addition to a super-strong urine smell, carried strong aromas of coriander, garlic and curry. It would have gagged a maggot.

When the guy was finally drained, the flight attendants were a bit pale, but the patient looked infinitely better. We cleaned up the area as well as we could, washed up and went back to our seats. I was exhausted, but Peggy was still burning.

"Not even a thank you. Not from him nor from the captain for saving his precious fuel. Jerks."

("Jerks" is, again, not the word she actually used.)

We had settled down and I was almost dozing when the patient's brother showed up. All of him. I hadn't realized how fat he was.

"Doctah," he said, "Ismael want you have."

He put the big ruby ring in my hand.

"Brudda thank you. I thank, too."

With a *salaam*, he waddled back up the aisle. I was so sleepy I was speechless until he was out of sight.

"Here, Peggy," I said, "you earned this, not me."

She took the ring and turned it over and over in her hand. Finally she said, "I'll be happy if we split this. You take it and sell it and send me half. I'd go with you, but I'm being met in LA."

"You'd trust me?"

"You said you are an honest liar."

"Well, all right. But I wish you'd take it all."

"Nope. Even split or I won't touch it. I loved your performance." She began to giggle.

I seldom argue with a pretty woman, so I let it drop, and forgot about it when I went through customs. When I finally went to have the ring appraised, the jeweler looked at me suspiciously.

"This a joke?" he asked.

"No, it was given to me and another person and I want to sell it and send her half."

"Maybe five dollars."

"What?"

"Maybe five dollars for the setting. The stone? It ain't. Glass. Poor glass at that."

"That son of a gun," I said. Gun was not exactly the word I used.

My problem now is how to tell Peggy. We both expected the ring to be worth thousands, and she'll be looking for half of some thousands of dollars. Should I send her $2.50 and expect her to believe me? I think not. Maybe I'll just mail the ring to her. Will she, when she finds out what it's worth, think I swapped rings on her? She knows my daughter-in-law, and God knows I don't want suspicions of dishonesty in the family. I guess I'll have to scrape up a couple of thousand somehow to send to her to keep my honest name clean.

If ever again a good looking woman asks me to do some charitable lying, you can bet I'll run like a scared rabbit.

The Bridesmaid Wore Stripes

I seem to gravitate toward odd characters and make them my friends. I said as much in the presence of two of my friends—they looked appraisingly at each other, then looked back at me and nodded.

I found Dolores' refuge for exotic animals when I was bicycling around in western Montana. Exotic animals intrigue me, so I stopped to look around. Dolores was impressed by my bicycle adventures and invited me in, where I was met by two of the biggest housecats I'd ever seen. They went romping about the house, over the sofa, onto the bookshelves like a pair of kittens. Dolores spoke sharply to them. They ignored her. She reached down and picked one up under each arm and shook them. They looked up at her and calmed down. She introduced me to Heather and Lem, two cougar kittens. I should have recognized them by the huge feet and the spots.

Their mother had been killed by a rancher, Dolores said, but he had captured the kits. Realizing he had no way to take care of them but unwilling to murder them, he turned them over to Dolores, who became their mother. She kept them in her house, and allowed them the run of the place. They were the size of very large housecats, but totally kittenish. They romped and climbed and chewed on each other like any kittens; and, like any kittens, they soon grew tired and lay down for naps. When they were hungry, they came mewing (more like "mrrrawing") to Dolores, and she fed them from bottles. Lem curled up on his back holding the bottle with four paws, while Heather cuddled on Dolores' lap. Like any babies, when they were fed they settled down for another nap.

As they grew they remained inseparable. When he was a little over a year old, Lem developed an ulcer that required a visit to the veterinarian. When Dolores took him from the cage, Heather set up such a ruckus that Dolores feared she would hurt herself.

When Dr. Jean Barth entered veterinary medicine, she specialized in a small animal practice, so she could help dogs and cats. She had never dreamed of the size of some of those cats. After Dolores' visit with two nearly grown cougars, Dr. Barth decided to make house calls to treat them. Not because the cougars needed it, but for the mental health of her smaller patients and their owners.

Dolores' biggest animals were a lion and a tigress. The big lion, Shorty, had been a character actor in films until he grew lame with arthritis, and the pain made him crotchety. As an actor he was finished, but in Dolores' loving care, he became a pussycat. The tigress, Lilly, had somewhat the same background, although she had a bad reputation of having mauled a trainer. In reality, Dolores said, Lilly had only swatted the trainer with her claws sheathed, and then only after extreme provocation. Of course, that the trainer wound up in the hospital with a concussion was almost Lilly's death sentence until Dolores intervened. Lilly shared Shorty's cage, and was as docile and friendly as he. On my first visit, Dolores and I hit it off so well she invited me to come in and play with them. I declined. My name is not Daniel.

Tara, on the other hand, was a lioness who had been raised in another shelter, and mistreatment there had made her suspicious of people. The first time I met her she rubbed against the wire beside me as I passed her cage. Her demeanor was so inviting that I reached down to scratch her ear. She spun, stood up against the wire net and roared.

"She's just playing," Dolores said. Yeah. Playing with my heart. It took several minutes to get the beat down to where I could count it.

Shawn was a rather young mountain lion. I have no prejudices against cougars myself, but there was something I didn't like about his attitude. While I was visiting, a family stopped to see the animals and a little girl of eight or so wandered among the cages. Shawn paced her, never taking his eyes from her.

"Does he like children?" I asked.

"Oh, yes, he certainly does," Dolores said. "With a side of fries."

161

Shawn had been kept in a pen in town, and had been a quiet pet until the local children had teased him through the fence until he became savage.

"I can't blame him," she said. I had to agree.

When Dolores met Hal, he was a broke, down-and-out ex-rodeo rider. He hired on as a flunky, but soon showed an affinity for the animals, and they for him. Even the somewhat dangerous cats allowed him in their enclosures, although they were watchful and nervous if anyone else was around, so no one really knew what thrall he held over them. Dolores knew. He loved them, as she did. In time their mutual interests ripened into romance, and Hal and Dolores decided to marry.

Since the animals had brought them together, the lovebirds wanted to include them in the ceremony. Hal and Dolores planned to be married in the big cage with Shorty and Lilly. They wanted Shorty to wear a black tie and "stand up" as best man, and Lilly to wear a ribbon and act as a bridesmaid.

Whom do you invite to your wedding in a lion cage? Eccentrics like yourselves, mostly. Normal people, when told of a wedding involving lions and tigers, found themselves busy on your wedding day. So among the oddball guests accepting was yours truly. I arrived a couple of days early so I could see the preparations. I was not about to volunteer to decorate the cages, but I did help with the peripheral stuff, working under Dolores' command.

Hal chose the minister, but neglected to tell him that the ceremony was to be performed in the cage with the big cats. When the Reverend Mr. White arrived, he looked equal to the task. He was over six feet tall and must have weighed a solid two hundred twenty pounds. Hal led him past Tara's pen and she, of course, lent her ear to be

162

rubbed. When she "played" with him as she had with me, the poor man fainted dead away. It appeared, for a time, that we needed another cleric—to perform last rites for Reverend White. Poor Tara looked downright apologetic— she hadn't meant to *kill* anyone.

When he revived, Reverend White proved himself either game, foolish or dedicated to his calling. Or perhaps all three. Although his knees still shook, he entered the cage with Hal and acknowledged the introductions to Shorty and Lilly. They, on the other hand, looked bored. When he returned to the house, I noticed that Reverend White gave Tara's cage a wide berth.

At the last minute, Hal and Dolores decided that the lion and the tiger should be chained far enough away so that they could not interrupt the ceremony. They wouldn't be bothered if a huge lion head entered the picture just as the groom was placing the ring, but they weren't sure of the effect on the Reverend Mr. White, let alone the human witnesses. It was good they were restrained. Lilly took a liking to the big yellow bouquet the bride carried, and tested her chain trying to get to that tantalizing morsel. Finally, Dolores was forced to hide the flowers behind her until the ceremony was over. When she threw the bride's bouquet, guess who got it? None of the other ladies chose to argue with the tiger.

I hear from Hal and Dolores often and they seem very happy. They don't plan to have children, though. Shawn the cougar must be greatly disappointed.

There are towns named Liberty, Freedom, Justice,
Amity, Peace, Hope and Harmony, but none named
Honesty. So says George R. Stewart in his *Names on
the Land.*

I wasn't looking for it—the maps said there were no
existing towns for miles. I was off the main roads,
looking for outhouses and other important old
buildings in abandoned town sites. The sign declaring I
had reached a town called Honesty and that it had a
population of five thousand and three completely
surprised me. Knowing some of the history of the area,
I was interested enough to investigate.

The first establishment along the road appeared to
have been, at one time, a general store, with perhaps

some rooms on the second floor. I parked and opened the sagging door.

"Come on in," a high-pitched voice called from the back of the store. The owner of the voice shuffled out and looked me over. He looked to have been maybe six feet tall at one time, but his present desiccated form stood no more than five feet seven.

"Can I get a can of Coke?" I asked.

"Sure thing. In the cooler there."

I took a can from the cooler. It was warm to the touch. The proprietor was peeking out the window at my license plate.

"That'll be three dollars." Three dollars for a warm can that at most should cost maybe seventy-five cents and be cold at that? Not wanting to start an argument in an isolated town where it might land me in jail, I paid him.

The phone jangled.

"That'll be Houston," the string bean said. Into the phone, "Yeah?" A pause. "No I don't want another goddam long distance service." He banged the phone down.

"I'm expecting a call from the Astros. I'm a pitcher and they'll activate me any day now."

If I'd been asked to estimate his pitches, I'd have guessed he could probably throw a forty-mile-an-hour fast ball.

I walked down the street looking for the rest of the town. All I could see was some dozen or fifteen buildings, so I thought there must be a lot more to hide the other five thousand people.

"Hi, there!" The voice boomed out of a shack marked "REAL ESTATE—LOTS FOR SALE."

165

The Realtor made a long speech telling how crops grew fantastically in Honesty's fertile ground what with the twenty-seven inches of rain. I looked around, and the soil looked to be two rocks for every dirt and was raising only cactus and an occasional sage brush. I guessed the twenty-seven inches of rain was all right, provided you counted all the precipitation for four years. I left him still talking.

Farther down the street another shack caught my eye. "GOLCONDA MINING COMPANY," it said. The man inside introduced himself as the sole owner of the Golconda. He wore a three-piece suit despite the hundred-degree temperature. The suit probably hadn't been shiny ten years ago.

"We're really booming here," the mine owner said. "Gonna be working three shifts of a hundred men. Can't get the railroad up here yet, so we'll have to truck the ore out. Got a dozen trucks on order."

He took me to the adit to show me the mine. You could see the end of the stope from the entrance. A hundred of Snow White's dwarfs couldn't have squeezed in there. Maybe there was another tunnel somewhere, but I still doubt it.

As we walked back to the mine office, we met a reeling bum.

"Meet Doctor Stillwater," said the mine owner.

"Hi," the good doctor replied. "Come to the saloon and help me celebrate."

"What are you celebrating?"

"Why, I've been on the wagon for two years today. Gotta celebrate."

I could hear the wagon he had fallen off of rumbling away down the mountain never to come back, I'd bet.

A big man with a sheriff's badge stopped us.

"You got that out-of-state car?" he asked me.

"Yes, that's mine," I admitted.

"It's illegally parked."

"Illegally parked? I didn't see a No Parking sign."

"City ordinance. Fine's thirty-five dollars.

"Thirty-five dollars? That's robbery."

"Don't want pay it? Might be called resisting arrest. That's a lot tougher fine."

I paid the S.O.B. He was probably the major source of income for the whole town.

I started back to my car, intending to flee while I still had my pants. A soft whistle called me from the only decent-looking place in town. The sign read "Justin Case, Attorney at Law."

Mr. Case motioned me inside.

"I suppose the sheriff fined you for something or other," he said.

"Yeah. Thirty-five bucks for illegal parking."

"Yes, I'm afraid our sheriff is not exactly honest," the lawyer said. "Furthermore, the whiskey in the bar is watered, the mine is a hole that's salted to lure investors, the store owner jacks his prices up times ten when an outsider comes in, and the teetotaller doctor hasn't drawn a sober breath in seven years. Oh, yes and there's the real estate agent." He paused and shook his head. "If I was a *real* lawyer, I'd get out of here, but as it is—"

With that, I ran to my car and got out of the town of Honesty as fast as I could. A town in which the only honest man is *pretending* to be a *lawyer* is just too rich for my blood.

Moose Encounter

Ted and I had canoed up the Pack River from Lake Pend Oreille in order to see the change of color in the early fall. We saw color changes, but not where we expected.

The Pack flows from the mountains northwest of Sandpoint, Idaho, turns south and meanders into the north end of Lake Pend Oreille. When the lake is at its summer level, the Pack is backed up for several miles, so it's a slow-moving stream. It loops and curves so much that sometimes a good arm (mine isn't) could throw a baseball from one loop to another, but a person would have to paddle half a mile to find the ball. Such a gentle, meandering stream is ideal for pleasure canoeists. Except for access. A golf course lies along the bank near the highway, but I haven't seen any signs welcoming canoeists. Once Ted and I managed to park near the bridge and portage in, but it was a long haul. More accessible is the boat ramp a mile or so farther along the lake shore, making for an interesting paddle back to the river. Of course, being on the open water, one is subject to the whims of that old fink Mother Nature, and will always have headwinds both ways.

Last fall, Ted and I wanted to see how the leaves were changing color along the river as the days shortened. We spent half a day exploring the loops and turns of the river, investigating dead ends and generally having a splendid time. As we neared the mouth of the river on our way home, we met a deputy sheriff in a power boat. Power boats are forbidden there, but we supposed The Law was allowed to have them.

"Say, have you guys seen a power canoe up this way?" the deputy asked.

"N-n-no. We haven't seen anybody except the g-g-g-g-g-golfers and th-th-th-they weren't on the river."

"Lady up here reported a powered canoe," the Deputy said. "She said it had paddle wheels on each side, and was making about twenty miles an hour and throwing a whale of a wake."

"N-n-never heard of such a th-th-thing. Was she sober?"

"I thought so. But you're right. That side-wheeler canoe would be too strange. Say, are you guys all right? You look kinda pale."

"W-w-we're OK."

"Well, have a good trip, fellas." The deputy turned his boat and sped downriver.

We didn't tell him the whole truth.

We had paddled up one of those dead end arms when we saw, ahead, a large brown something wallowing in the water.

169

"That can't be what it looks like," I said.

"What can't it be?" Ted asked.

"It looks like a manatee, but there surely aren't any of those hereabout."

"No, there sure can't be. Let's get a closer look."

We approached the "something" and were close enough to see a broad, hairy hump when the moose raised her head from the bottom.

"Oh. A moose. Let's get closer to get some pictures."

We eased past the cow and found ourselves between her and the shore.

"Maybe we'd better get out of her path," Ted said.

"Oh, she doesn't seem concerned. Why should we be?"

"BECAUSE HER CALF RIGHT THERE ON THE SHORE JUST CALLED TO HER."

Mama started for us just then, and we both changed color from ruddy tan to pale gray. We paddled rapidly away, but Mama gained on us every second, and she didn't look like she was planning to pose for pictures.

"Faster!"

I don't know whether she was swimming or tip-toeing along the bottom, but Mama still gained.

"Faster! Faster!"

I think that's probably when the observer saw us. Our paddles may have been going so fast they looked like side wheelers, and I know my canoe never threw a bigger wake.

Mama Moose soon decided we were no longer a threat, and gave up the chase. We slowed down and paddled down the river, not trusting ourselves to speak until we met the deputy.

Ted's color slowly changed back and his normal ruddy tan had returned by the time we loaded the canoe on the car. I don't know when my color came back. It wasn't something to be talked about.

The Coming Of Autumn
1992

It is unusual for North Idaho and western Montana to have long sieges of really hot weather, but this year temperatures stayed in the high nineties for days on end during most of July and August, with occasional breaks for the high eighties. A thermal high stayed around, pushing the cooling thunderstorms we expect in the summer northward into Canada. The Forest Service warning signs, day after day, placed the fire danger at extreme, its most dangerous level. Although the nights were cool, the house failed to cool enough from the heat of one day to ease the heat of the next. Even the basement, normally insulated from the summer heat, warmed up to the high eighties.

We welcomed the cold front that came through around the twentieth of August with open arms. The front brought significant rain, and some fine cool weather. Too cool. In Ronan, Montana on the twenty-third of August, I woke to snow. Tiny flakes among the raindrops changed to the huge feathery flakes that, in winter, presage a heavy, wet snowfall. The shock was too much for the area. It was fall from then on. Oh, the temperature went back to the nineties, but it just wasn't the same. Suddenly, the shadows were long at noon—we hadn't noticed them growing longer. Evenings cooled early, and swimming in the lake suddenly seemed uninviting, even though the water was still decently warm.

The trees noticed. A few had begun to turn—some always hurry the season—but after the August cold snap all the vegetation took on a subtly autumn look. The lilacs across the street turned deep red and golden yellow and began to lose their leaves. The maple and ash and poplar trees began to change in earnest, and most of them were very soon in full color and dropping their leaves. A maple tree showed a little color one day, turned bright green and gold and red for a day, then became a brilliant yellow, and finally, beginning at the top and moving down, stepped out of its summer raiment like a woman stepping out of a loose robe. We all felt that it was too soon.

In the previous year, the warm weather held on until the middle of October. Many of the trees were still green and full when, a week or so before Halloween, a sudden drastic temperature drop quick-froze the leaves on the trees so that the apple trees and many other normally bare trees stayed green through the whole winter.

With each shift in the weather, the wind blew dust and fallen leaves in an impromptu ballet. Rain showers alternated with brilliant sunshine from deep blue skies. The blackbirds wheeled in flocks, and long vees of geese passed overhead. There is a sadness about fall, but there is a special beauty too. The summer's promise of harvest is fulfilled by the garden's bounty and the reddening apples on the trees.

We moved here to enjoy the change of seasons. We even drove to Montana a few times to look at the changing colors there, where the cottonwoods along the rivers are in all shades of green and gold, and the tamaracks on the high ridges are splashes of gold among the dark evergreens.

Yes, winter is coming, but with it will come another special change, another kind of beauty.

Alberton

You've experienced it. Sometimes when you're in a familiar place you know something is different, something's *wrong*, and you can't exactly say what. As I drove east past Alberton, Montana, heading for Missoula, I had that uneasy feeling, so strong I turned around and drove back to Alberton hoping for some clue to my anxiety.

The glare of an all-white landscape added to my disquietude. Alberton is off the freeway a bit, so I hadn't been there in several years. Someone seemed to have overdone the whitewash; the buildings were pure white, and so were the rocks.

Red's Bar and Grill seemed a good place to inquire. The bartender sported a bushy white beard and a head of curly white hair. Hard to tell where one left off, since his skin was almost as white as his beard. After howdies, I asked if the boss was around.

"I'm him," the bartender said.

"How come this is called Red's?" I asked.

"That's me. Red O'Shaughnessy."

"Were you a redhead when you were young?"

"Whadda ya mean, when I was young? I ain't but thirty years old."

"Something scare you white-headed?" I joked.

"You're an outsider, ain't you?"

"Not exactly. I grew up Charlo, but I live over in Idaho now."

"Reckon you didn't hear about our train wreck."

"I read in the Spokane paper that a train wrecked here this spring. Seems I read they evacuated the town."

"Yup. Except a few of us stayed. And that's what happened to my hair."

In the early spring of 1996, Red told me[13], the media kept busy in Montana with their extended and superfluous coverage of the Freemen in Jordan and the capture of the alleged Unabomber in Lincoln. When a Burlington Northern train wrecked in Alberton and several cars of chlorine were dumped, little coverage was given to the event outside the Pacific Northwest. Sometimes the media are so busy with one story they miss (or simply neglect) another, more fascinating one. Or maybe some stories just don't fit the editors' views.

The railroad moved everybody out of town—everybody, that is, who would move—and put them up in Missoula. Then the "experts" set about to clean up the mess. How do you clean up chlorine? The gas is poisonous and caustic to the skin. Whoever was in charge decided the best way to handle the situation was to chemically change the chlorine to bleach. Well, you know what bleach does. All the color went out of everything. The rocks were white, the trees were white, the buildings were white.

"The white hair—oh, the chlorine! Did the bleach ..."

"Yeah. Bleached me clear out. Ever'body else who stayed in town bleached, too."

The batwing door slammed open, and we both turned. The newcomer's face and hair were as white as Red's. The bartender reached over the bar to shake hands.

"Good to see you, Sal. Say, this here's—what'd you say your name was?"

I told them my name, but left off my profession.

"This here's Sal Angeleri. Sal runs purebred Black Angus cattle on the bench above the river west of here a few miles. Sal, Dick's right interested in what happened

---

[13]These are not exactly Red's words. I have cleaned them up considerably to retain the family flavor of this book.

with the train wreck. I know the chlorine got to you. Did you lose any stock?"

"Didn't really *lose* no stock," Sal said, "but how the hell can I sell Black Angus when me and them goddam cow critters are all bleached out plumb white. Look at me! Hair was as black as them cow critters, and now we all look like a bunch of goddam albinos."

I shook my head in commiseration, and ordered him a beer. A man with that much trouble deserves a friendly gesture.

We talked for a while, Sal complaining about how hard it is to round up white cattle among white rocks and white fir trees. After a time, I drifted out and wandered up the street. A booming voice stopped me.

"Dick Hoskins! Hey, paleface, don't you know your old friends?"

The speaker came toward me with his hand held out. The long, snow-white braids tied with pigging string, and the bow of his legs, looked familiar; but it took several seconds for me to recognize the seamed and lumpy face. I turned his hand over and shook it.

"Charlie Thundercloud! How's the Indian Activist business?" I've known Charlie since we were kids. He didn't advertise his Indian ancestry then, and we just knew he was a bit more deeply tanned and could run a lot faster than most of us. Charlie became a champion bronc rider and a pretty good bare-knuckle fighter, but he'd hung up his spurs and made a career of denigrating everything done by the white man, although usually when he referred to "white man" he meant the United States Government. "What you doin' off the reservation, Charlie?"

Charlie's face, hilled and valleyed like a Montana landscape, became sober and threatening like his name.

His eyes flashed at me as he grasped my hand. I had never seen him look so angry and yet so worried.

"It's sickenin', Dick, sickenin'. Might as well leave the reservation for good. Can't say a word against the goddam white man anymore."

"Why not? Who's stopping you?"

"I can't say nothin' cause now, goddammit, look at me. The white man really got to me and now I *are* one."

It was true. Charlie is now the whitest man I ever hope to see. Too bad. He was a damn sight better looking as an Indian.

I was getting into my car to leave, when a thought struck me. That was it! The river. That was the reason for my misgivings. The normally placid river all the way from St. Regis to Alberton was roiling, boiling whitewater. That must have been very strong bleach.

I haven't been into the town of Alberton lately, although I notice the river is no longer whitewater down at St. Regis. The Indians are agitating to take over the National Bison Range, so I suspect Charlie's back in business. Think I'll drop by and cuss the old boy out.

Marvin

Marvin wasn't sure when he became "Old Marv" but he knew it was long before he even began to think about retiring. When he finally hung up his badge, he had even begun to think of himself as Old Marv. He still retained his amicable relations with the Highway Patrolmen that he had nurtured along and formed into the finest force in the state, and even volunteered whenever the Department found him useful.

When Clara died, he felt completely at loose ends. He took up fishing seriously and, along with his volunteer work, it kept him busy enough to dull the loneliness. He bought a fishing car, the pickup Clara had never wanted. Since he expected to be alone in it most of the time, he chose only the minimum options, although he did select the driver's side airbag. He'd seen the advantages at a dozen wrecks.

Today Marvin was just at the wrong place at the wrong time. He had just filled his tank with gas, when the wild-eyed young hoodlum ran from the station waving a gun. He ordered Marvin into his truck, and jumped into the passenger seat.

"Drive!" the gunman said.

Marvin knew better than to resist. He had been on both sides of the business end of a pistol while a patrolman. He started the pickup and rolled smoothly out into the traffic. His professional memory made him want to insist the hoodlum buckle his seat belt, but he held his counsel. No use antagonizing him unnecessarily.

"Where to?" Marvin asked calmly.

"Get on the freeway. No tricks."

"Which way?"

"East. Head for the mountains."

Carefully obeying all traffic laws, Marvin drove through the signals to the on-ramp and entered freeway traffic. The nervous gunman looked in every direction, but kept the pistol pointed at Marvin's head.

"Drive legal, stay in the speed limit," his passenger ordered.

Marvin watched the speedometer needle and held his speed to the designated 65 miles per hour limit. The gunman relaxed a little when they were a few miles from town, and it was apparent to both him and Marvin that they were not followed.

"Go over the pass to Montana," the gunman said.

"That's two passes and about seventy miles," Marvin told him.

"Yeah. Be in Montana in a little over an hour." The gunman grinned. "Lots of places to get rid of you there."

His tone chilled Marvin.

As he started up the grade in the lesser of the two passes, Marvin noted a Highway Patrol car parked at the chainup area. That was common. He'd stopped there himself before driving up the winding road, hoping to control speeders who were not aware of the sharp turns. He drove past the turnout with his eyes forward, but a glance told him the patrolman was his own son. Oh, God, he thought, don't let Chet tail us.

The patrol car pulled onto the freeway right after they passed, and soon was gaining on them. Marvin noticed, but said nothing to his captor. Soon the young man turned around and saw the patrol car.

"Shit," he said.

BLAM!!

The gunman shot out the back window of the pickup, then turned around and began firing at the patrol car.

Marvin was glad to see the patrolman back off, leaving space enough to make the gunman's pistol ineffective.

As they topped the pass, Marvin examined his options. The fellow was concentrating on the patrol car, but Marvin knew he was not muscular enough to wrest the gun away. Best he drive, and not try anything stupid.

As they approached the bottom of the pass, the gunman noted the exit sign.

"Take the next exit," he said.

"Gotta slow down," Marvin told him. "The road tees there. Which way you do want to go?" The exit was approaching fast.

"Go right. No! Don't get off." The gunman turned to look back at the patrol car.

Well, Marvin thought, the punk can't make up his mind. He doesn't have his seat belt on. I could arrest him for that. Can't make up his mind? Well, I'll just go between. Barrels of water were stationed at the point between the exit and the freeway lane, protection for drivers who tried too late to take the exit. Marvin prayed his airbag would work. The first water barrel exploded in front of him, he felt a huge hand press him against the seat, then he was twisting, tumbling and then blackness.

He was next aware of terrible pain in his legs, and he tried to rise to look around. The gunman sprawled against the windshield, his head at a crazy angle. The gun was not to be seen.

"All right, don't move." It was his son's voice, addressed to the passenger side of the car. The gunman didn't move—he never would again.

Some time later, Marvin heard the sirens and was aware that he was being moved ever so carefully. Chet stood near his stretcher, crying.

"Dad, what could I have done?"

179

"You did just right," Marvin whispered. "How did you know to follow us?"

"Dad, when did you ever drive past a parked unit and not stop? Something had to be wrong. Then I heard an APB that a pickup had been hijacked, and I put two and two together. But why did you crash?"

"He'd have killed you and me too. Only thing I could do. Hell. I had an airbag and seat belt. He had nothing. I expected to at least jar the gun out of his hand. Guess I hit harder than I expected. Poor bastard."

Advice Column?

Virginia Crouse
Has married a louse
Who beats her and causes her harm.
I say she should feed
The guy poison weed
And bury him out on the farm

Tiger by the Tail

If you haven't been to Castle Crags State Park south of Mount Shasta on Interstate 5, I suggest you might want to stop there. The crags are as spectacular as the Grand Tetons, but on a smaller scale.

The Park provides a trail that brings you to several scenic points. At  one point, the trail leads to a jutting cliff, and a fence protects the foolhardy from the cliff edge. A sign on the fence warns people to stay on the trail. Do so.

The point just outside the fence was too tempting. Being an old hand at rock-hopping, I ignored the sign, and positioned myself on the rocky point to take some really fine pictures. After the first picture, my camera rewound and I had to change film. I twisted around, laid the camera down and reached for the film in my pocket. That's when the fun began.

The foot I depended upon to hold me against the rock lost the normal tension and slipped. And I slid down the rock face. Not fast, but too fast to scramble back. Fifteen feet or so down the face, my feet encountered a ledge and I came to a halt. Before I could call for help, a snarl to my left warned me, and I saw there, clinging to the narrow ledge, a very large and apparently angry mountain lioness.

There aren't supposed to be any lions here, was my first thought. My second thought was lost when the lioness swiped at me with a claw, lost her footing and managed to regain a claw hold with only her front feet. As she struggled to regain the ledge, my tenuous handholds let go, and I began to fall. The lioness twisted toward me as I fell, and I slid down the back of a squalling lioness. Her lashing tail hit me, and grasping for straws, I seized the end of the tail. You have heard of having a tiger by the tail. Well, I had one, and the other end was caught on a narrow rock ledge, but holding fast, thanks to those massive lion claws. I hung there contemplating what to do for all of two seconds before my engineering mind began to operate.

Let's see. The cliff's only forty feet or so above the scree, and I fell fifteen feet to the ledge, and now I'm hanging down from the ledge one large mountain lion length, including her tail. When I looked down, I could see the jumble of rock was only two or three feet below my dangling toes. I could think of no future use I might have for a mountain lion so I let her go. The lioness thanked me by scrambling up to the ledge, then bounding off toward the forest. I walked back to the road, back up the trail to get my camera and back to the car where The O'Reilly had waited for almost an hour. I told her I was wandering around getting good pictures. She'd never have believed the truth.

Epiphany

I woke to the crunch of gravel outside my tent. Possibilities flashed through my half awake mind. Cow? Moose? Bear? I sat up in my tent and peeked out. There in the light of the half-moon I saw Bigfoot dragging my canoe. I opened my eyes wide and my mouth wider to yell, then realized it was only Don, out there clothed in nothing but his gray body hair.

"What's up, Don?" I asked.

"The river."

We'd camped on a gravel bar, knowing that a dam in Polson controlled the river level, but expecting no more than a six-inch rise in the river.

For years, I dreamed of taking my canoe for a long, slow float down the Flathead River from Dixon, Montana, to Thompson Falls. It should take about three days, I thought. Three days of loafing, letting the river do the work, not a care in the world, exploring the islands and the old, old ranch buildings on the north side of the river, camping out on the river bank. Oh, I knew there was a small section of whitewater, but I could see it from the highway, and it looked canoeable. Trouble was, no one else had that particular dream until I met Don. He and I just hit it off right away. We both enjoyed canoe trips and welcomed some adventure along the way.

Don hadn't gotten around to dreaming of floating down the Flathead, but when I told him my dream he said he thought it was a big enough dream for two of us. For his share, he said the world is full of taxi drivers. He had hiked much of the Pacific Crest trail and when he came out and wanted to go back to his car, he'd go into a bar and make it known he'd pay to have someone drive him back to where he'd parked his car. Never failed to get a ride, he said. So we'd park the car in Dixon and catch a "taxi" back from Thompson Falls.

We met on a Monday. That Thursday we were in Dixon, with our tents, sleeping bags, ice chests, cameras, more food and drink than we could possible use, and a bright outlook on life. We loaded up the canoe, left our car in Dixon and we were off. The river was just as I had dreamed. We floated along, only paddling enough to keep our course straight, or to cross the river to look at something on one bank or the other. The weather was perfect, with clear skies and temperatures in the low 80s. What more could you want?

The old buildings were as interesting as we'd expected. We guessed they've been there for 80 or 90 years, but their sides were logs and someone had kept the roofs in good repair, so they were as good as new. It appeared they served as horse barns, maybe in the winter. I believe the close-up pictures I took of Don in his old wide-brimmed hat leaning against the log barn are classics.

The islands were a different story. The river level had been up and down so the bushes at the shore of the islands were in water, and approaches that were clear of bushes were a foot deep in mud. We cruised around one or two islands, then, disappointed, decided we'd just float on by. When the sun began to touch the trees, we looked for a place to camp. The islands were inaccessible, the highway ran close to the south bank, and the north bank was too steep to climb, let alone put up a tent. We paddled around in some inlets where we scraped bottom, and finally chose a gravel bar that rose a couple of feet above the water. That seemed high enough. Our privy would be the bushes on another island twenty yards or so away.

We discussed the best spots for our tents.

"You choose first," said Don. "It's your trip."

After a token argument, I set up my tent in a spot where the rocks were smallest. Mine is a two-man tent, made in Korea for two awfully small men. There's barely room for me. We warmed some hot dogs and beans on Don's grasshopper stove and dined royally. Amazing how the open air improves the flavor of plebeian meals. When it got too dark to walk around safely, we said goodnight and crawled into our tents away from the mosquitoes. Next thing I knew, Bigfoot.

"The paddles were floating when I got out here," said Don. "I think I got the canoe up high enough, if the river doesn't rise more than six more inches. If it does, we're in deep doo-doo."

"Is everything else out of the water?" I asked.

"Everything but your tent," he said.

That brought me out to look. Fortunately, my tent floor is more or less waterproof, and extends up the sides a couple of inches. So did the water. I pulled up the stakes and dragged the tent to the highest ground on the bar. We went back to bed, but promised ourselves we'd sleep lightly, just in case the dam at Polson opened up even more in the night. We needn't have worried about sleeping soundly. An owl nearby started calling.

"Hoo-hoo. HOO."

From somewhere up a canyon, another owl answered.

"Hoo. Hoo-hoo. HOO." They called all the rest of the night. I suppose they were saying, "Catch anything?"

"No, how about you?"

Of course when I moved my tent from the bed of small gravel, I found the biggest rock on the whole damn island, and it wound up under my hips. No matter how I turned, that darn rock gouged me. I tried moving my mattress, but the rock seemed to move with it. Sometime around four o'clock, I fell asleep. Daylight came at five.

The day was another fine one. We coasted along having a great time. At one point, we saw some kind of animal splashing in the water all the way across the river. A cow? No. We couldn't imagine a cow doing that. A moose? Well, maybe. We paddled over that way until the animal got a look at us, ran up the bank to the trees, then stood on his hind legs and looked us over. No, not a Bigfoot. Just a little old black bear. We saw cutthroat trout in the river, so we supposed he was fishing, albeit unsuccessfully.

A few miles farther downstream, we came around a bend and saw what looked like the splashing of a shallows ahead, except the shallows appeared to be standing on edge. Strange. As we came closer, we realized that the "shallows" was a wall of water about two or three feet high where another swift stream entered the river. I couldn't remember any creek that size, but when I got a look at some landmarks I realized we had come to the confluence of the Flathead and Clark Fork rivers. No wonder there was a wall of water. These are two pretty big streams, and they flow at a good rate. We passed the junction in the calmer water on the far side of the river.

As we floated through the town of Paradise, we agreed that our course on the river was much more a paradise than the environs of the town. The river flowed faster here, and late in the afternoon we floated through the back streets of Plains. would you believe that no one noticed? No brass band, no ticker tape parade, no nothing. Nearest thing to ticker tape was the business page of the newspaper a whirlwind blew around us.

The town of Plains maintains a very nice campground, but we decided to continue to a wilderness camp. Near sundown we were getting nervous. The shore on one side of the river consisted of rocks the size of automobiles. We crossed to the other side to find an eight foot bluff with a cow-pasture fence at the top. We cut the inside of a bend and found flat ground with tall grass at the foot of such a bluff, but the water needed to rise only a foot or so to flood the area. Wiser now, we chose to look elsewhere. Directly across the river there seemed to be a sandy island. We paddled in that direction and found that because of the flow of the water around the bend, paddling across the river was paddling directly upstream, and we were making no progress at all. Finally we tired and gave up, and moved diagonally across the river. As if in answer to a prayer (Don's, I guess. Wasn't mine.) we coasted below a sand spit into a backwater lagoon. This time, we pulled the canoe up the six-foot sand bank and found a level sandbar as big as a football field. We deemed that large enough for our two tents and set up camp. Don cooked supper in the dark.

We expected a quiet night—both the road and the cows were across the river—but our luck was bad again. This particular lagoon was the local singles bar for a Great Blue Heron population. By morning, that population was endangered—if we could only have gotten our hands on them. All night long we heard the Great Blues calling, "Grrawwk! Grrawwk!" We supposed that means, in heron, something like, "Nice legs!"

On the third morning, the river ran more rapidly than before. When we first launched, we could look downstream and actually see the slope of the water, although the ripple was very small. After a few miles, the river slowed and we had to paddle to make any appreciable progress. Then we began to hear a roar, and knew we were approaching that whitewater that I had seen from the road. We landed above the rapid, and looked it over. One bank was a jumble of rocks the size of automobiles. We crossed and examined the other side. The bank was rocky cliffs. We had a choice. Shoot the rapids or walk the shore and let the canoe ride down at the end of a rope. Neither of us had whitewater experience, so we opted for lining the canoe down.

We looked for the rope that we had brought for this purpose, then remembered leaving it in the car. Oh, well, we had a length of nylon sash cord which certainly was strong enough. We tied it to the forward thwart and eased the canoe down while we clambered over those huge rocks along the bank. Lining turned out to be so easy we berated ourselves for chickening out. We were sure we could have paddled through the rapids. Oh well, now the road to Thompson Falls was an easy float. Ha!

A mile or so farther along, I began to hear a roaring in my ears. I thought my blood pressure was acting up, until Don commented that there must be a second rapid. There was. We examined this one long and hard, and finally decided we could line down the rocky side. One of us would let the line out to almost its full length until the other, downstream, could catch the line; then the first guy would clamber past him and catch the rope downstream. We must never, ever let the rope be out of the hands of one or the other of us, or we'd never catch the canoe.

Don took first watch, but he ran out of rope before the line got down to where I could reach it. I looked out there in the river as the canoe went sailing by with the line lazily following. If I wanted my canoe back, I'd better act. I plunged into the river, swam out and caught the line, and struggled back to the rocky shore. The river and I had a tug-of-war for the canoe. Like a maverick steer, the canoe took off for the middle of the river, and rolled over on its side. If it capsized, I knew I couldn't hold it, and I planned to jump in holding the rope and float downstream with it.

After an eon or two, the canoe righted itself and tamely came back to my side of the river. I steered it down to an eddy and sloshed down to it. Both my hands had deep cuts where the line had passed, but I felt good that I'd managed to hold that bronco canoe.

"Did you see that?" I asked Don.

"See what? I didn't see anything. I was too busy falling down on these blasted rocks."

"Well, the canoe was out there clear over on its side, and if it didn't tip over in there, I guess it isn't going to tip over at all." Events proved I will never be successful as a fortune-teller.

We guided the canoe into an eddy and tied it while we ate lunch. That was the smartest move we made that day.

We agreed that the best thing to do was to paddle the canoe out into the current, then steer her downstream. What we neglected to discuss was the direction the canoe should point when we got into the current. Don worked hard to get the prow upstream; I worked as hard to point the prow downstream. As a consequence, a wave generated by the rapids won the contest. The unrollable canoe rolled over.

The water was very pleasant, and we laughed at ourselves as we floated the inverted canoe down to the foot of the rapids. We righted the boat and we took stock. We had done an excellent job of tying the gear down with bungees that morning. I had lost one "water sock" and my kayak paddle, and Don had lost his sunglasses. We bailed the canoe dry, and thinking that the worst must be over, edged the canoe carefully out into the current. Our spirits were high. Even though the canoe had rolled, little of our gear was wet. Little did we know.

Another mile or so downstream, we heard a sound we did not want to hear—this time, the rapids' roar was audible around a bend in the river. We ran for shore on the rocky side, and scrambled over the big rocks to reconnoiter. Big trouble. The river dropped fifteen or twenty feet over some fifty yards or so, creating some *real* whitewater. This was too daunting even to line down.

Fifty yards from the water on the rocky side of the river lay the open pine forest. We considered portaging over those rocks; but, having found we could barely carry our own weight over them, we agreed to try the other side of the river. We crossed and pulled the canoe up onto the shore. It seemed awfully heavy, and investigation showed why. Our sleeping bags were thoroughly soaked. So was everything else in the canoe. The sleeping bags suddenly weighed fifty pounds each. We took time to wring some water from them and spread them on the rocks to dry while we planned our course.

Seventy feet or so above the river ran the main line of the railroad. We thought that from that level we could scout the river easily. We began the climb to the railroad in good humor, and ended it panting and puffing louder than the old steam trains. If we kicked a rock loose, it rolled all the way to the canoe.

Don opted to walk downstream along the track to see if he could find a place to put in, should we portage. Since it was mid-afternoon, I chose to scout the highway in case we had to give up. I knew the road was close to the river— I'd driven it many times. I climbed the railroad cut and worked my way up the mountain. I found the road about a half-mile from the railroad, and followed it upstream for a time, remembering that we had seen it and the railroad close together that afternoon. The area where the two were close was a disappointment. The railroad fill was composed of large boulders, and portaging up was impossible. I found an area where the slope up from the railroad to the road was minimal, and marked it in my mind.

We met at about four o'clock. Don's report was inconclusive. He had not seen more rapids, but he hadn't seen a good place to get to the river to put the canoe back in. My report wasn't good, but we discussed the merits of going downstream to an uncertain fate, or going upstream and packing out. We agreed that the best thing to do was to get our gear up by the railroad, whichever way we intended to go. We started with the canoe.

I have a portage cart for my canoe, so we strapped it on and moved the canoe up those seventy feet to the railroad. Should have left the cart off. The wheels caught on the rocks and weeds and brush, and sank into the loose dirt. With the canoe up, we discussed our plight, but agreed the situation wasn't entirely hopeless. Then we slid down and began hauling up the gear. I carried the ice chest up that ninety-foot cliff, then went after miscellaneous gear. I quit counting after the twelfth trip up the one-hundred-twenty-foot bank. We left the sleeping bags until the last, hoping they had dried out. They hadn't. The water in them must have lowered the river a foot or so. When we had, at last, reached the railroad, two hundred fifty feet above the river, we caucused. The sun was touching the trees. It was time to quit this trip and pack out.

We loaded everything in the canoe and discussed what we'd do if a train came. If we had plenty of time, we'd lift the canoe off the track. If we had little time, to hell with the canoe. We started up the tracks, upriver, to a spot I'd discovered half a mile away where there was minimal bank on the railroad cut. Our ears were tuned to the sound of a train, but the bump, bump, bump of the canoe wheels on the ties required that we stop frequently and listen. We encountered no trains.

191

We hauled the canoe off the tracks, and began moving gear up the hill. Fifty feet higher, someone had bulldozed a fire break, leaving a sort of road. Once we got to the fire break, the slope up to the road was relatively easy. Getting gear that first fifty feet was the problem. The slope was such that it took two feet and one hand to climb, leaving one hand to carry gear. We took the canoe first, all the way to the fence at the highway right of way. Then we began hauling gear up that seventy-foot bank to the fire break. After climbing that hundred feet a couple of times, we sat and tried to catch our breath. What a couple of old fools like us were doing out there packing stuff up from the river came up in our conversation. Our only answer was: "It was there."

After my fifth trip up the hundred-and-fifty-foot slope, I began slapping mosquitoes and commented it would be dark soon. Don was ready for me.

"I'd feel better if you'd go get the car while I pack the rest of this stuff up," he said.

"Why don't we just bite the bullet and both work and get it all up?"

"Then you'll still have to go after the car, and by then it will be late and what little traffic there is will be done with."

"Well, I guess you've got a point. Listen. When I get a ride—if I get a ride—figure it will take me about two hours to get to Dixon and back. After about an hour and a half, shine this big flashlight on the trees here. It's so dark I'll never find you if you don't."

"Here, take this." Don handed me a paddle. "Now put this life jacket on and go stand by the road."

I did as I was told. Car lights appeared in a few minutes and a large sedan went zipping past. Oh, well, there'll be more. Ten minutes later, two pickups went by, one after another. Oh, well, there'll be more. Then the second pickup did a u-turn down the road half a mile, came back, u-turned again and stopped beside me.

"I know where you've been."

"Guess it's kind of obvious, isn't it?"

"Get wiped out in the rapids?"

"No. We didn't try those rapids. Decided to pack out. I need a ride into Plains."

"Get in. I'm going there. Got a car in Plains?"

"No. Figured I'd offer to pay somebody to drive me to Dixon."

"What'll you pay?"

"Oh, twenty-five dollars."

"I'll take you."

And he did. He cut the drive time from Plains to Dixon by a third. I just closed my eyes and let him drive. In Dixon, he said good-bye and sped away.

The moon wasn't up yet, and in the dark I could see approaching cars for a long, long way. Taking a lesson from my taxi driver, I drove faster than I should have, and arrived back at our rendezvous in just over an hour and three quarters. I stopped on the road near where I was sure we had come with the canoe. There was no light in the trees.

"Don?" I called. No answer. Well, maybe this isn't the right place. I drove on up the road, checking at each likely looking-place. No Don. Five miles up the road I knew I was past where I should be, so I turned around. On the way back, I recognized a building that I'd seen when on my reconnaissance mission. Ah. Just a bit down the road from here. And that was where I'd stopped at first. This time, I turned off the motor and sounded the horn. The light came on in the trees beside the road.

"I just got so tired I'd have to sit and rest for ten minutes or so," Don explained. "Guess I finally went to sleep. But I got all the gear up here."

We began loading the car. We couldn't believe the amount of traffic that came by. Almost every car stopped, and those that didn't slowed enough so the driver could ask if we needed help.

"We're in Montana," I told Don.

We refused help until we were ready to load the canoe. By this time, we were so tired we both sat at the edge of the road to dread the task a while. A car pulled up nose to nose with ours. A small wiry man of forty-five or so came over to us. His accent was definitely Irish.

"Do ye need any help?"

"Well, we could use some help loading this canoe."

"Let's do it."

Don and I were very little help with the canoe—our new friend lifted the canoe by himself. When we got it tied on, he asked if we were all right. Yes, we said, and thanked him again and again. He shrugged off our thanks as if he had done nothing unusual. We were in Montana, for sure.

I offered to pay for a meal in Plains, but Don said he was too tired to eat. I offered to pay for a motel, but Don just wanted to get on home. So I drove the hundred miles home like a zombie.

Don summed up our trip this way.

"It was a religious experience," he said. "Two days of heaven, one day of hell."

I cannot add to that.

Disease Prevention

We are addicted to variety catalogs. Well, maybe not addicted, but we might as well be. New ones appear in our mail every day. We have bought a number of handy gadgets which we never have found at any regular store. When we found a pottery garlic baker, we sent for it immediately. Barbara, our daughter-in-law, makes delicious garlic mashed potatoes, using instant potatoes and stirring in garlic that she has baked and then squeezed from the cloves. We thought that, with this gadget to cook the garlic, we too might approach Barbara's recipe for potatoes. We didn't know the proportions, but we guessed a head of garlic would be more than enough for the amount of potatoes the two of us could eat. I didn't want to spend the time it took to heat the oven and bake the garlic in the oven, so why not use the microwave?

Because...

Put a little oil on the garlic, the instructions said, and bake in the oven or the microwave. No times, no temperatures, no microwave settings. I set the microwave for a couple of minutes on high. That didn't seem to cook the garlic enough, so I tried a couple more minutes. Presently, smoke began to trickle from the microwave. I opened the microwave door to a rolling mass of smoke issuing from the garlic baker. I lifted the lid and found a brisk fire burning at the center of the garlic head. I rushed the whole thing to the sink and poured water over the smoldering mass. Too late. The smoke filled the house, and the whole place reeked of burned garlic.

Within a week or so, we tamed the odor in most of the house, but no matter how many times we wash the microwave, the stench of scorched garlic fills the kitchen every time we turn it on. Not only that, we washed that smoky garlic baker in the dishwasher, and now the dishwasher smells of burned garlic. We can't always taste it on the dishes, but we live with it every day so maybe we've become inured.

I don't know where the garlic baker is now, but I suspect I could track it down by the smell should I want it. But we gave up using it because we found that Betty Crocker makes fine garlic potatoes in a box.

Garlic is supposed to prevent disease. I wonder what the effects of garlic smoke are. I suspect that no self-respecting germ will enter our house for months. Maybe no self-respecting person, either.

We sure are healthy, though.

Blue Plate Special?

Nathaniel Pegg
Eats an ostrich egg
Each morning when down at the zoo.
He wonders, does Nat,
Why he's getting fat
On one egg and some toast. Wouldn't you?

BRAG '97

I had a bike wreck last winter and tore up a knee so I didn't ride BRAG '98[14]. I managed to drive a private SAG vehicle, although I was on crutches some of the time. Maybe it was for the best. The 1998 ride was hot and dry—we had no rain at all.

The 1997 ride was anything but dry. Some riders exaggerated and said they rode in rain every day, but I doubt it. I only rode in significant rain for four of the seven days. What do I call significant rain? Well, for example, the day Sandra and I hid out at noon, we stopped only because we couldn't see ahead for the rain. When the rain started that day, the weather was warm and a little shower felt good. As the intensity of the rain increased, I began to chill, even though the temperature was in the

---

[14]For more about BRAG, Bike Ride Across Georgia, see "BRAG Days", More *Montana: Tall Tales, Damn Lies and Otherwise* page 176.

high eighties, so I got out my slicker. Said slicker acts like a sail, and the only wind in the sail was caused by my forward motion. Pedaling against wind is one thing. Pedaling against the wind with a sail is another. I finally tied the slicker down with my butt-bag strap, leaving the contents of the butt bag to the rain. I wasn't the only one whose possessions got soaked. Some of the restaurants along the way said they hadn't seen a dry dollar bill all day.

After our lunch stop, we rode through rain that continued off and on, as did my slicker. Then, in the afternoon, the rain began in earnest. We had no choice but to keep riding—there was no suitable shelter, and the rain looked like it would continue forever anyway.

We were riding up a hill on which the rain was a veritable river running down the roadway. The water was so deep, a whole school of salmon passed us going upriver. I commented to Sandra that I knew why those salmon were going upstream, but was damned if I knew why we were.

"Well, don't expect me to spawn with you when we get to the top," she snapped.

The rain eventually slowed and stopped, and we were able to take off our rain gear. Good thing, too, because when the sun came out the temperature rose alarmingly. Late in the day, I began to tire, having fought the slicker and the rain and the heat all day. I really slowed down, especially on the hills. I didn't mind when that vulture sailed around looking me over. I didn't mind when he landed on a fence post to get a good look. But I drew the line when he perched on my handle bars, cocked his head and asked plainly, "Are you moving or not?" I beat him off with a bike-lock chain, and despite my exhaustion, high-tailed it to camp.

Grits

When Georgia residents assured me that peanuts grow underground, I said, "Sure they do," thinking I knew a good lie when I heard it. But it turns out they were telling the truth. After they bloom, peanuts burrow underground to develop. Well, strange things happen in Georgia.

Take grits. I have been fond of grits ever since I met them in North Carolina in 1946. To keep me going all day on a bicycle, give me a breakfast of grits and eggs, with some butter and cheese. I have done some research, and found out some interesting things about my favorite breakfast.

Grits trees can be found throughout the southern states, and grits grow on the burr from this tree. One grit grows on each spike on the burr, and a single burr from a good grits tree will produce a quarter to a third of a cup of grits. To harvest the grits, one must knock them off the burr without breaking off the spines, since eating grits spines will cause a person to talk slowly and say "all" for "oil." Nowadays, the grits burrs are rolled gently around on a polished stone surface, from which the grits can be collected easily.

It was not always so. Before polished stone was used, the grits burrs were taken to the top of Stone Mountain (near Atlanta) and rolled down the mountain, and the grits were collected by sweeping the stone surface. Stone Mountain is not polished stone, and when the grits were swept from its faces, a minute amount of stone dust was collected also. From this stone dust came the appellation "grits."

And to think I learned all this while breakfasting with a couple of lawyers in Atlanta.

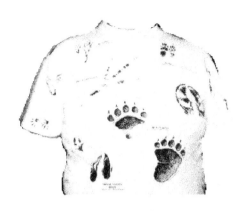

The Shirt

A few years ago, I took a solo canoe trip to a lake hidden high in the Selkirk Mountains. The summer had been hot, the woods were dry, and I knew wildfires were a possibility. Lightning had set many fires in the past few weeks, but all had either burned themselves out or been squelched by more recent rain. Thunderstorms were again brewing, so I paddled miles along the lake looking for a place to camp where I'd be protected from both fire and lightning. Around much of the shoreline the trees grew almost to the water. The scenery was beautiful, but the setting was unsafe for camping. In other places, the shore was jumbled rocks at the base of a cliff. I was getting arm-weary when, near sundown, I found an ideal camping spot. On a gravel-bar peninsula, a recent forest fire had burned down to the edge of the lake and left a small meadow between the water and the burn. The cliffs and snags around me would take any lightning strikes, and the burned area would stop a fire.

I pitched my tent, cooked supper, drowned my fire, doused myself with insect repellent and lay down outside the tent so I could watch the stars. I slept. Too soundly. I didn't even hear the thunderstorm but woke only when a sudden heavy rain sluiced over me. Rolling over, I could see a bright glow on the ridge beyond the burn. Lightning had started another fire, but I felt safe with my pre-arranged backfire.

Before I could pick up my blankets and move to the tent, I heard a rumbling sound, and suddenly I was drubbed, tumbled, pounded and otherwise abused. I covered my head and hoped my tormentors, whoever or whatever they were, would go away. When the thundering stopped, I looked around for whatever had punished me. The t-shirt I wore gave me a clue. Various tracks indicated that the forest denizens had stampeded from the fire, run through the wet ashes of the burn and right over my reclining body.

Next morning, bruised, stiff and sore, I packed my gear and paddled slowly back to the campground where I'd left my car. I took me half an hour to load my canoe onto the car, and I swore I'd never go canoeing alone again.

Being a responsible citizen, I stopped at the Ranger Station to report the fire and my experience. The Ranger took one look at me and asked what had happened. After I told him of the fire and of the beating I'd taken in the night, he came around his desk and examined my shirt carefully.

"Hmmm," he said. "I knew we had black bear up there, but I didn't know we had grizzly." He went over my shirt naming various animals that had tramped on me in the night. Finally, I took the shirt off and we stenciled on the name of each track. He thanked me for taking a census in the area, something he hadn't had time to do.

That shirt is still one of my favorites. People often ask how they can get one like it, but when I tell them they'll have to camp out by a burn and let the animals run over them in the night, they seem to lose interest.

A Writer's Fantasy

I'm driving along US 95 north of Worley, Idaho coming back from a canoe trip to Windy Bay, and I see a Jeep Cherokee in the ditch. A well-dressed guy stands by the back of the car waving me to stop. I say to myself, "What the hell," and pull over. He tells me his steering went out, and wants a ride to a telephone. He has an appointment in Spokane, and needs to reschedule that as soon as he can.

As I drive toward Coeur d'Alene, he seems nervous and worried, so I ask about his appointment.

Turns out it's with an author and he comments how temperamental authors are. I laugh and comment that we certainly are. He wants to know why I say "we."

I tell him I write humor and damn lies about my boyhood. He says he could use some humor about now, and asks me to tell him one of my stories. Instead, I reach in the back and pick up a copy of my book *Building Character:Tales from Montana (And Other Damn Lies)* which I always have along.

He opens it, begins reading, and shortly he's chuckling and then giggling. He closes the book and asks how much I want for it. It's a damaged copy; glad to find an appreciative audience, I tell him he can have it.

Only then does he tell me he represents a network TV producer and is going to see someone in Spokane, but he thinks my stuff has potential for episodes of a series and will try to sell the idea to his producers. There may be a long-term contract in it, he says.

And you say a person shouldn't pick up hitch-hikers? You do if you want to have decent fantasies.

Grandpa's Cookies

I offered a grandchild a cookie.
He made a face and shrugged.
"I don't like that kind."
He turned back to his toys.

I offered another grandchild a cookie.
She took it, but, saying not a word,
She skipped away
To share it with her friends.

I offered a third grandchild a cookie.
He smiled as he took it and said,
"Only one? Can I have some more?"
I gave him more, until, sated,
He turned and walked away.

I offered yet another grandchild a cookie.
She said, "Oh, goodie. I'll get some milk for us."
She broke the cookie and gave me half.
So we sat and laughed together
And shared what each of us had.

I offered a grandchild my love...

About the Author

Dick Hoskins was born in Iowa and raised on a farm within the shadow of the Mission Mountains in the lower Flathead Valley of Montana. After service in WWII, he graduated from Gonzaga University in Spokane, Washington. An Engineer, he was sentenced to many years exile from the Northwest. His work carried him to both the east and west coasts of the United States before he retired to live in Coeur d'Alene, Idaho.

Dick and his wife, Dorothy (The O'Reilly), have ten children and more grandchildren than he wishes to count.

Much of Dick's material reflects his farm upbringing and his western values. And his father's admonition: Never let the truth get in the way of a good story.

Also by Dick Hoskins:
More Montana:Tall Tales, Damn Lies and Otherwise, (206 pages, $10.95)
Building Character:Tales from Montana (And Other Damn Lies), (203 Pages, $9.95)